Born in London to a Swedish mother and English ..... , Anita spent her childhood moving between the two countries. She met her husband when she was eighteen and they laid down roots in sunny Dorset to raise their four children. With the children now grown and flying the nest, and the family expanding, Anita divides her time between tracing her ancestral roots across Ireland, England and Scandinavia, and writing in her nature filled garden with her cats.

For more information on Anita, on her writing and books, read her blog on anitagriffiths.blogspot.com, follow her on Instagram anitaegriffiths and Twitter@anitaegriffiths and join her on Facebook @anita.e.griffiths (Anita Griffiths Writer)

By Anita Griffiths

The Cobbled Streets saga

Cobbled Streets & Teenage Dreams

Close Your Eyes

Beyond the Ironing Board

The Box

Short Story Collections

Zara

The Box

Anita Griffiths

For my family

Xxx

In memory of my dear friend Wladyslaw Myslak

(1911 – 1992)

A gentle man, a huge inspiration and a keeper of stories

Chapter One

She was here again today. She's alright really, I suppose; quite sweet, if it weren't for her incessant questions. She wants to look at all my treasures, to rifle through my book collection for something she might like to read, to inspect my kitchen cupboards, always asking questions. Questions, questions, questions. I can't be doing with it.

"Can I call you *auntie*?" she had said.

"No!" I replied. Not deterred, she studied my face, scrutinising every inch, right up close. I could feel her warm breath on my cheek; her infantile, snuffled breathing stirring something long since repressed in me.

"Can I call you *grandma* then?"

That hit a nerve. I didn't like that. I shook my head, shooting her a look that should have warned her to stop. She didn't.

"Why not? You look like a grandma. I had a grandma once. She's dead now."

Excellent. Just what I want to hear.

"How old are you?"

"I'm eighty-five. How old are you?"

"I'm seven." She sounded so proud. "My grandma was fifty-eight when she died. She was old. You must be ancient!" I couldn't help but smile at her stare of wonder. I had given her something new to think about, to speculate.

"Where are your grandchildren?"

She caught me off guard. My smile froze.

"I ... I don't have any."

"Why not?"

Her mother, Annika, stepped in, reaching for her hand.

"Kära lilla; sluta nu."

1

I know enough Swedish now to understand that she was being told to stop with her questions. Annika gave me a smile of apology as she took her daughter through to the kitchen. I shouldn't be so intolerant; at least she shows an interest. I find her name endearing; Majbritt. Pronounced My Brit, which is ironic of course because she is so unlike a Brit! I wonder what the xenophobes make of her name. At least she and I have that in common; we are aliens in this quaint, quirky and sometimes very unforgiving, country.

When I first arrived, I was welcomed with open arms, or so I thought. Until the whispers started. Amidst the genuine sympathy and empathy towards my tragic plight, I saw through the plastic smiles; the guarded, bristling indignance at the interest my arrival had stirred. I get it; another mouth to feed, another head to count when the air raid sirens cut through the still nights. Another child to keep safe when so many were already in danger from the monsters in the sky. But I was desperate. Angry, yes. Frightened, very. Lonely, infinitely.

It didn't take a genius to work out what had happened to my mother, or my aunt and uncle. I had seen my father, face down in the street. I saw the red, pooling about his lifeless head, his hair wet with it. His beautiful, always immaculate, hair that smelled of violets. It was at that moment that Uncle Jusef had snatched me up and silently run through the back streets, his clammy hand covering my mouth in case I screamed out. I wanted to scream but Papa's brutal murder had struck me dumb. For quite some time, actually.

"Kristabel, would you like more tea?"

I smiled and nodded at Annika, glad for the distraction from my musings. I hate looking back but the older I get, the stronger the urge is. To revisit, to linger, to reignite treasured memories etched in my heart. It's so hard to do without reawakening the demons that lie dormant too. So tightly interwoven, robbing me of childhood warmth. Of sunny days long gone. Sometimes a smell, or even a colour, will bring back a rush of feelings. Chrysanthemums – Mama's favourite. I know traditionally tulips are synonymous with the Dutch but for my wonderful mother, always chrysanthemums. That intense, vibrant orange; those were her favourite. Not quite burnt, not quite garish; just on the cusp of either. The smell when you rub the stiff, upright stems – that is my childhood, in one inhaled breath.

I waved from my armchair when Annika called goodbye. Majbritt rushed over and hugged my arm, inadvertently wiping her nose on my sleeve.

"Goodbye Kristabel! See you tomorrow." She turned as she ran back to the door, nearly slipping over on the polished floor. "I love your name, it sounds like a kiss!" She waved, earnest blue eyes fixing on tired hazel ones. She really is a poppet. Despite all her questions.

Arthritis is the bane of my life. I don't complain though. I know I'm lucky to be here, lucky to have such a comfortable life. I used to feel guilty, intensely so, but nowadays I appreciate the comfort. I embrace the things that money can buy. The heating is on constantly. I have the finest, plumpest quilt on my bed and the softest sheets. I have a daily help – Annika – just for the little things I no longer can manage. Well, I probably could manage some of it but not without pain or ending my day with such an unbearable ache in my bones. The type you can't escape, can't walk away from. It's like labour pain, only in your joints rather than your pelvis.

Yes, I do know about labour pain. And yes, I do have grandchildren.

Annika and Jan are my neighbours. They live directly below me in our beautifully refurbished Georgian building. Each apartment has been meticulously designed for modern living, yet keeping its original charm and many original features, such as the ornate architrave and ceiling roses. Annika and Jan moved here from Sweden three years ago but into our house, only two months ago. Annika is very unassuming, eager to help, hard working. She's a qualified doctor but chose to leave her job to raise Majbritt. She works as a dinner lady at the school and as I said, spends an hour a day with me. Jan is a whizz kid in computer software or programming or some such, which if I understand correctly, is the modern day equivalent of my late husband's job in the civil service. I never really understood his job, only that it was well paid and he travelled a great deal. That's how I met him. On one of his business trips. He was stopping off in Amsterdam on his way back to London. It sounds corny but I think he was sent to me by some other worldly force. He arrived just at my very lowest point in life and he instinctively knew I needed someone strong to take over the burden I was carrying alone. He was my saviour. But not my first love. And not my first husband.

"But what does it mean?"

"It doesn't *mean* anything, really. It's just a pretty thing to wear. Don't you have pretty jewellery to wear?" What was I thinking? She's only seven.

"Mamma says if it doesn't have a meaning, do we really need it?"

Yes, Majbritt was here again, armed with an endless list of questions. Today, it was the contents of my jewellery box that came under scrutiny. She was examining the brooch nestled in her hand. A beautiful cameo in Wedgewood blue with a silver edging, studded with tiny pearls. She was right to be enchanted by it; it truly is a treasure. I debated her question, trying not to smile at the adult sentiment being voiced by a child. When I was a child, I hoarded treasures, regardless of their meaning. Majbritt was waiting for an answer.

"Well, in that case, it's *meaning* was to tell me I was loved. This was a present from my husband, Howard."

She studied me for a moment in that unnervingly intrusive way. She is a child determined to delve into my very soul and root out my secrets. She has no filter, she has no boundaries. Just bold curiosity. It courses through her veins, I can see it. She'll make an excellent investigative journalist one day.

"Where is he?"

"He's dead."

"Because he was ancient?"

I laughed out loud, nodding. "Yes, my little one, he was quite ancient. Ninety-two, in fact. Much older than me." I chuckled at her serious face, hugging the memory of him in my head. Sensing I wasn't sad, she mimicked my chuckle and shuffled a little closer to me on the sofa.

"Tell me about Howard," she demanded. I shrugged.

"What do you want to know?"

She gave my question some thought, slowly tapping her chubby index finger on her pursed lips. Her eyes lit up.

"What was his favourite ice-cream?"

It's been two years since my beloved Howard drew his last breath. Here, in our bedroom. It wasn't expected. Well, at our age of course it *is* expected but what I mean is, he wasn't ill. There was no prolonged death, no lingering goodbyes. I woke up one morning but he didn't. I sat in bed next to him for an age, holding his hand. Then I went and made some tea, poured us both a cup, got back into bed and drank mine, all the while stroking his arm. I remember saying things like, *'it's alright, Howard, it's okay.'* I think I was trying to reassure myself of that. I mean, for him it is okay; he's not the one left behind. He's not the one who had to deal with everything. Yes, he had sorted out all his affairs, all the legalities of leaving this life, all the business of a funeral and the extortionate expenses of it.

Why are weddings and funerals so unbelievably expensive? Most of us get married, and we all die, so why aren't they the two things that are made easiest and least costly. My friend's granddaughter got married three years ago. It cost them just over forty *thousand* pounds! I saw the photos – it wasn't that amazing or ground-breaking. Just another beautiful wedding in their local church and a reception in one of London's smarter hotels. I certainly couldn't see what they spent forty thousand pounds on. And now there's a baby on the way and they still haven't saved enough for a mortgage. They live in a rented flat, out of central, so the commute to work is ghastly for them. The pressure must be unbearable. Whoever saw a market in weddings and funerals and decided to exploit it to the hilt, needs a good shaking. I feel sorry for this generation. The expectations to achieve are so great, so much so that they have lost perspective. The sense of belonging, of community, of pulling together – they'll never have that. That's gone.

Howard's funeral went by in a haze. Lots of people turned up, most I knew but some, I had never met before but obviously they had known Howard. Through work. Even though he had retired some twenty years previously, they still remembered him and wanted to pay their respects. Lots of suits. Lots of black. In retrospect, I wish I had been brave and suggested mourners wore some colour but Howard was quite a traditionalist, so the occasion really suited. It was a fitting departure, as so many said on their way out of the crematorium. We drank his health in his favourite restaurant, ate the food that the staff he and I knew so well had prepared. They did a wonderful spread. And the anecdotes were a comfort to hear. But when it was all done, when everybody had gone and I came back to our apartment – alone – there was something new to deal with. The silence. We weren't a noisy pair but we did like to talk. Constantly. About anything and everything. And Howard would whistle, or hum. Or sometimes, sing. We played records. We danced in our living room. And the kitchen. Right up til his last day. It was more of a hang-on-and-sway kind of dance but that's what happens when joints get older, knees less willing, feet stiff from years and years of punishment. I think we under-estimate feet. They work so hard for us and it goes unnoticed. We just take them for granted. It's not until they stop working as efficiently that we suddenly notice them. Howard always insisted on the best shoes, for that very reason. '*Look after your feet*,' he would say, '*and the rest will slot into place.*'

I polished all of his shoes, the day after the funeral. Laid them all out to air by the window and let the polish soak in. Then I aired his suits. His thick winter coat, his tweed jacket and his older tweed jacket that was replaced but he hung on to anyway. I asked him, some years ago, why he still had his old tweed jacket that had definitely seen better days; he didn't wear it anymore.

7

"It brought me luck once and I don't ever want to tempt fate by getting rid of it," he said. I just smiled and kissed him, silently thanking him for that gentle reminder of the day we met. He had been wearing that jacket, and being the true gentleman that he was, had offered it to me as I sat huddled by the canal in the drizzling rain. I was in such a state, emotionally, that I hadn't even noticed it was raining.

Eileen dropped by, the day after the funeral, with some cake and to check that I was alright.

"Oh good, you've made a start then," she gushed, her eyes wide, obviously uncomfortable at the sight of Howard's belongings.

"A start?"

"Yes, it's good. Very healthy. Shall I get Jack to drop it off at Oxfam later? He can bring the car round, save him lugging all those bags on foot." She smiled; her earnestness was beginning to annoy me.

"I'm not giving any of it away, Eileen!"

"Oh, then ..." she spread her hands out in question, looking around the room.

"I'm just cleaning his shoes and clothes, ready to store. In the wardrobe. Where they belong."

"But ..."

"But nothing," I countered.

"You need to move on, Kristabel," she urged in a hushed tone. Seriously; very annoying.

"Tea?" I resorted to the age-old notion that tea is the answer to everything, and depending on how you say it, can shut up even the most persistent of people. It's a warning, it's a *'I'm too polite to say it but don't pursue this any further'*. She took the hint. The thing is, I'm not *wanting* to move on. I'm waiting to join him. Oh, I don't want to die – of course not

8

– but I didn't want him to die either. And life with〈
no life at all. It's an existence. It's a patient waiting game.
trouble is, I've never been a very patient person.

"Tell me some more about Howard," Majbritt demanded
again. She was picking up where we'd left off the day before.
Her white-blonde hair had been fashioned into two plaits on
either side of her head, in the style of her favourite ragdoll,
Pippi Longstocking. She clambered across the sofa and rested
her elbows on the arm, leaning towards where I sat in my
armchair.

"What did he look like? What was his favourite colour?
Mine's blue; what's yours?"

"Mine is lilac; it always has been."

"What's lilac?"

"It's a lovely soft colour, in-between purple and pink. Like
your dress, only much, much paler," I said, pointing to her
purple, corduroy pinafore. She glanced down at what she was
wearing and nodded her approval.

"And Howard's favourite colour was also blue; like you."

She gasped in delight, beaming.

"I like Howard! It's a shame he's dead."

It's funny but I was starting to warm to her. It's taken a little
while to adjust to having such a young companion but she has
this wonderful, unabashed, forthrightness about her. I like
that. I wish I had been like her. I wish I had asked more
questions when I was her age.

"Fetch that thick, white book over there," I instructed,
pointing to the solid, mahogany unit on the other side of the
room by the door. I slowly got up from my armchair and
moved over to the sofa, watching Majbritt carefully take the
photo album from the lower shelf. She paused to survey what

...'s a handful of books – the
...ookcases in Howard's study – some
of vases, a mass of framed photos, a
...graph albums and our extensive collection
...e of place, our very modern record player. We
also ... ...D player and radio but that's in the kitchen. We
loved co... ...ecting records; we loved music. We used to
frequent this little shop on Carnaby Street. I mean, it was the
height of fashion back then; you were really 'cool' if you
bought your records on Carnaby Street. And we never parted
with any of them. It made Howard chuckle how much people
started to rave about old records when they made a come-
back not that long ago. It's the thing now; artists release their
songs on vinyl as well as CDs. It did mean that record players
made a resurgence and we were able to find this wonderful
piece of technology. Our records never sounded that clear
before. I still prefer it to the CD player but Howard was quite
a fan of technology and gadgets. He liked remote controls and
devices he could talk to. It amused him. He taught me how to
use the internet and how to work the incredibly expensive
computer he purchased. He insisted I took a course, which I
did about twenty years ago but I learnt far more from just
watching him. I rarely use it now though, apart from for
online shopping.

Majbritt heaved the heavy album onto my lap and settled
down next to me, smoothing down her pinafore and
straightening her wrinkled, yellow tights with white daisies
on. Satisfied that she was comfortable, she turned expectant
eyes to mine. I smiled.

"This is my wedding album," I told her. She clenched her
hands with excitement, grinning. "We were married on

October twenty-fourth, in nineteen sixty-six. A long time ago."

In fact, Howard died just a few weeks before our fiftieth wedding anniversary. We had a party planned; nothing too grand, just friends and family. Howard's sister, our nieces and nephews, our old neighbours. As it turned out, it's where we held his wake instead, and the menu he and I had planned together was served that day.

Annika poked her head round the door. I could tell what she was thinking; yesterday had been the twenty-fourth of October.

"Mamma, come and look! It's Kristabel's wedding!" Majbritt moved closer to me, making room for her mother. Waiting for her to sit down, she nodded for me to continue.

"Why do they look like that? Why isn't there any colour?" She frowned at the photos.

"Because colour photos were a very new thing then, and hardly used. I do have lots of colour photos of us when we're a bit older. I can show you later."

I set about pointing out who was who, talking about my dress and what colour the bridesmaids dresses had been. Majbritt gave a delighted smile when I told her they were lilac.

"Mamma, lilac is a soft colour. Like my dress but paler," she said, repeating the explanation I had given her earlier. Annika smiled, nodding.

I lingered over the photo of just the two of us. He really was a handsome man. Tall, well groomed, always so polite. And calm. That's the first thing that had struck me about him; that air of calmness. And in control. He was a cross between Cary Grant and Sean Connery; dark haired, dark eyed. Puppy-dog eyes that seemed to melt when he smiled. Older than me by

11

nine years, he was forty-one when we met; forty-two when we married. Unlike me, he hadn't been married before. Unlike me, he hadn't had children. But he had witnessed the horrors of war. He joined up in nineteen forty-two, when he turned eighteen. He saw the liberation of my country. He marched through the streets with his battalion, greeted by hundreds of Dutch civilians throwing flowers at them. I listened to him, enthralled, as he told me that story. I could visualise it all so clearly. Although the streets I was visualising hadn't been destroyed by endless bombing in my head. By the time Howard had arrived, the country I had known and loved was a mere shell of its former self. Some parts worse than others. He didn't talk about the war but in our early days he told me that story more than once, each time adding a little more detail. He knew it brought me comfort, a strange bitter sweet joy. He hadn't been there to save my family but he had been there to save their land of birth. Our heritage.

"Did Howard like the cinema? I love the cinema. We saw Incredibles 2 – I loved it!" Majbritt was happily hugging my wedding album. Annika had gone back into the kitchen to make tea.

"Yes, he did. Although he loved opera more. Me, not so much. But I went along with him. We did everything together, you see."

"Like a best friend?"

"Yes, Majbritt, just like a best friend. He was my best friend, always."

"Gemma's my best friend but I don't think she'll mind if you are my best friend too. Shall we …?" She held out her little finger to me. I was bemused, so she took hold of my little finger and linked it together with hers.

"What does this mean?"

12

She shrugged. "I'm not sure but now we are best friends forever and you can't break it. I think. That's what Gemma said, anyway."

"Ah well, if Gemma said that, it must be right then," I smiled.

"So now we have to make bracelets and then we're done. Oh, and I have to give you my cheese strings but that's tricky because I give them to Gemma."

"Did Gemma tell you that rule, too?"

"Yes. I don't think it's real but I don't mind. Cheeses strings aren't that nice anyway," she whispered, glancing towards the kitchen. The benefits of cheese was obviously an on-going debate with her mother. "What else did Howard like to do?" The way her mind flits makes me smile.

"Well, we both adored the theatre. We went every week. And some of the theatres in London are so beautiful that I'd go just for the décor."

"What's décor?"

"It's the way the building is decorated, inside. Look at my light," I pointed up to my elaborate ceiling rose. "Imagine that, but fifty times bigger and painted in gold. Then imagine it on the walls and the balconies, and imagine the seats – like at the cinema – padded and covered in a deep red velvet. And the floor is carpeted. It's all very beautiful and ornate."

Majbritt was enchanted. She clapped her hands together. "Can we go?"

"Yes, we can," I said without hesitation. "I was younger than you when my parents took me to the theatre for the first time. I shall never forget it."

"Your parents? Where are they? Are they dead, with Howard?"

13

I stopped short. Annika called Majbritt's name from the kitchen, a warning tone in her voice. Majbritt rolled her eyes dramatically and gave an exaggerated sigh.

"Mamma thinks I ask too many questions." She waited for me to disagree.

"You do!" I laughed. Her face dropped. "But I don't mind," I added quickly. I took her hand and led her over to my unit. We looked at the photos. I have many, in varying sizes. I reached up and carefully lifted down a large frame. Of heavy pewter, it has a detailed scrolled edge, with an intricate weave of roses and leaves through it. Wiping the thin layer of fresh dust from it, I handed it to her.

"This was my family. My mother, father, Elise – my mother's younger sister, Jusef – her husband. They lived with us. My mother's parents. And these are my father's brothers – Markus, his wife, Eva. Sander, his wife, Hannah. Abel and his wife, Maria. And my father's sister, Ruth and her husband, Daniel. And here are my cousins, that's all of us, sitting on the floor."

"Which one is you?" she interrupted. I pointed.

"I am the one with the ridiculously huge ribbon in my hair! I had to have the biggest, I had to have the brightest. This was Hanukkah and we all wore our best clothes, so of course, I had to wear my best ribbon."

"What's Hanukkah?"

"It's a special time, like Christmas. It's a festival of light. We have gifts and we light candles," I tried to condense the explanation to as few words as possible.

"Like Sankta Lucia, you mean? We light candles and sing and eat biscuits. Like that?"

I nodded. "Yes, like that."

Satisfied, she ran her finger around the frame, murmuring words in Swedish, before passing it back to me.

"Shall I sing you some songs?" It was clear I had no choice but I was happy enough to listen. I sat back down, holding my photograph close to my chest. I closed my eyes as Majbritt sang songs I had never heard before in a language I didn't understand. But I understood the sentiment and I found it comforting.

The photograph had been the last thing my mother had hurriedly packed into my bag before I left. I only had a small case and somehow it had survived the journey unscathed. The glass had been thicker and stronger than I had expected. It was the only thing I had as a reminder from home. That, and my tatty old rabbit. I keep him safe in a box in my bedroom. He'd had a faint, lingering smell of my home, of the perfume that pervaded the walls. A mix of my mother's expensive scent, of candles, and cooking. But despite my efforts to preserve it, the smell faded over time. The memories did not.

Chapter Two

I answered the door, wondering who would be knocking so early. It was Annika.

"Good morning, Kristabel!" She held out a potted poinsettia, offering it to me with a radiant smile.

"For me?"

She nodded. "Yes. Just a little something for you. A late gift for your anniversary."

"Oh!" I was taken by surprise, not sure what to say.

"And I wondered if you would like to come out with us today. I am taking Majbritt to the park – well, the indoor play area – and they have a little café there. I thought we could treat ourselves to some coffee and cake. Or tea, if you would much prefer it."

I smiled. Her English and the way she uses it reminds me so much of a younger me when I came back to England again in sixty-six. I still talk like a walking dictionary sometimes, I know it. A little clipped, a little precise.

"I would love to, thank you. What time?"

"Eleven o'clock, if that suits you?"

I nodded and she did a double thumbs-up as if encouraging a child, before hurrying back downstairs. Closing the door again and taking my new plant through to the kitchen, I glanced at the clock. I had three hours to get ready. That should do it. Silly, I know, but I have become a bit of a recluse since Howard died. I suddenly realised that aside from my weekly taxi trips to the cemetery, it has been over two months since I last went out anywhere; since Annika and Jan had moved in, and Annika has been on hand to fetch bits and bobs for me. The bulk of my shopping is done on-line and delivered by a polite young man named Darren.

I patted my hair down for the umpteenth time. I still have plenty of hair; it hasn't thinned or lost its will to curl in all directions. Howard and I both had dark hair once upon a time and as we grew older, it turned a steel grey. I don't think I will ever have that lovely silver white that Eileen has, but then again, she was always fair haired.

I opted for a navy woollen skirt and matching Chanel style jacket, with a fuchsia, soft silk blouse. I carefully pinned my cameo brooch onto the jacket and slipped on my ugly but comfortable navy shoes. Once upon a time, I wouldn't be seen dead in anything but stiletto heels. Even my slippers had had those cute little kitten heels – and pointless bits of fluff that had been all the rage.

Majbritt gasped dramatically when I answered her impatient knock.

"Kristabel, you look like a pretty princess! Mamma, can I wear a dress too, instead?" She pulled at her multicoloured leggings, grimacing her sudden disapproval at what she was wearing.

"No, Majbritt. You can't play in the ball-pit in a dress, can you? No, so … you look very fine also."

"You do," I agreed. "I would rather be wearing your leggings but they didn't have my size," I added. She laughed, eyes sparkling, and ran down the wide staircase to the front door. Realising I was taking my time, she ran back up again, then skipped back down and then up again, all the while chatting about the pigeon that had landed on their bathroom windowsill and peered in at her while she was cleaning her teeth. I was quite exhausted by the time I reached the door.

It was a surprisingly quick drive to the park, taking the back-route that most London commuters seemed not to favour. I had rarely visited the children's park; there had never been a need to. We had wandered through it on occasion, as an alternative route home from one of our many walks, but the indoor play area was a new entity. I seemed to be in a minority of not knowing its existence; the place was heaving with excited, loud, young children, and parents who'd had all the energy drained from them. Half term was certainly taking its toll. Despite the sheer volume of people, we found a table in amongst an assortment of parked pushchairs, with a good view of the smaller ball-pit where Majbritt had rushed off to. I held on to the bright pink trainers she had unceremoniously deposited on my lap before dashing off, loudly greeting children she recognised. I watched her effortlessly join in with their game and slowly but surely take charge, shouting orders as they raced to shovel as many plastic balls up the tube slide before the next child came careering down it. The laughter it induced was infectious.

Annika returned with a brightly coloured tray laden with coffee, tea, orange juice, pastries and biscuits. She called to Majbritt, indicating to the juice, then waved and laughed as Majbritt shrieked with surprised joy when plastic balls shot out from the slide, followed by an equally surprised boy. He jumped up and helped to shovel more balls, ready for the next unsuspecting child.

Like her daughter, Annika has typically Swedish looks; blond-haired, blue-eyed, with a trim figure that seems to need no maintenance whatsoever. I watched her wolf down a Danish pastry, then reach for a biscuit to dunk in her coffee. She flashed me a wide smile.

"Fifty years of marriage; that's a wonderful achievement, Kristabel."

"Yes, I know. So sad that that's a fact nowadays."

"So, thirty-three when you got married? A late starter. Mind you, so was I. I was thirty-two when I had Majbritt."

"And you don't plan for any more, or...?"

"We'd like to but I had a miscarriage. Twice, in fact." She caught the look on my face as I turned away, her stark admission hitting home. "You too, huh?"

I nodded reluctantly. "Well, stillborn actually."

"Oh no, that's even worse! I'm so sorry, Kristabel. That must have been awful for you. How did Howard react? I'm sorry, I'm prying." She held her hands up in apology. I shook my head.

"No, no, it's okay. I just ... haven't thought about it in a long time. It was before I met Howard. He was my second husband, you see."

We fell silent for a while; she, absently stirring her half-empty cup, me, picking at crumbs of pastry on my plate.

"It was a girl. I named her Lena, after my mother. She's buried in Amsterdam, in a pretty graveyard not far from where I grew up." We stared at each other for a while, neither knowing what to say, both feeling each other's grief. That maternal ache that doesn't ever pass. That gnawing speculation of what might have been. A sudden shriek of laughter made us both turn, my eyes automatically seeking out Majbritt. I refused to dwell, refused to wonder. But she made it so hard for me to do.

"Majbritt is a lovely girl, Annika. She is delightful!"

"I know. She is such a bright child. And to be so at ease with her new home, new language. Bilingual at her age – she's wonderful."

We sat watching the children play, in companionable silence.

"Did you and Howard not want children?"

19

Somehow, I knew that would be her next question. I paused, not sure I wanted to answer but I did nevertheless.

"Well, yes, I would have loved to have children with him. But there were complications you see, after Lena, so the decision was taken away from me. I had to have major surgery and ..." I left the sentence hanging in the air. What more could I say? I'd had major surgery immediately after her birth; a problem with the placenta breaking away had left us both very vulnerable. For my baby, it meant she died during birth; for me, it meant without the surgery I would have bled to death. Part of me wanted to join her, to slip away, but I had a stronger reason to stay. To fight for my life.

When I explained to Howard that children were not an option, I'd felt relieved to be honest, although I could never have voiced that. I just couldn't have coped with that fear, that dread of another stillbirth. Of losing another child. So I was relieved that we had no choice. Howard accepted it. He never once mentioned wanting children. I do know though, if we had been given the chance to, he would have doted on them, loved them, unconditionally.

"So, if she – Lena – is buried in Amsterdam, when did you come over to England?"

"Nineteen sixty-six."

"When you married Howard?" She smiled when I nodded. "So, it must have been a whirlwind romance then." I could see her doing the maths.

"Not really. I met him in the spring of sixty-five, in Amsterdam. He flew over whenever he could but it was difficult being apart for so many weeks at a time so I moved over here as soon as he proposed." I made it all sound so simple, so idyllic. It had been far from that. My mother-in-law had been outraged that I had thrown Niels – my first husband

20

– out of 'his' home; it was a pokey flat that we both paid the rent on and at the time, I earnt more as a secretary than he did as a waiter, so I paid most of the bills. When she discovered about Howard she was even more outraged. Apparently, it was okay for her darling son to have affairs. It was my job as a dutiful wife to forgive him and be more understanding. But for me to meet somebody else once our marriage was over, was unforgivable. I couldn't wait to leave.

"So you were there during the war. That must have been … difficult. How did you survive? I thought …" she paused, then shook her head. "I'm sorry, I realise I'm asking too many questions but my grandmother had a sheltered life through the war so I'm curious to know what it was like."

"Don't be sorry. It's just … Howard never asked questions and I never told him things. He guessed, and he knew some of it but at the time, we just focused on the future. Neither of us wanted to linger in the past. The war destroyed us all, in so many ways. He was at the worst of the battles, you see. Nothing good comes from remembering that."

She nodded, apologising again. "I read Anne Frank's diary at school; we all did. So sad. She was from Amsterdam too – did you know her?"

"No I didn't."

"Really? That's a shame. Why do you laugh?" She looked surprised at my reaction.

"Because if I had a pound for every time somebody has asked me that, I'd be very rich indeed. There were around eighty thousand Jews in Amsterdam before the Germans arrived, so it's not really *that* surprising that we never met. Anyway, she was older than me, so I probably wouldn't have noticed her." I smiled, feeling a little guilty at laughing at what she had thought was a valid question. "But to answer your

21

earlier question, I survived because my uncle managed to get me out of the country. Just in the nick of time, as it happens. I think I was one of the last ones to get out safely. I was brought over here in May nineteen-forty. My family …" I shook my head and gave a resigned shrug. "They didn't survive."

Annika's eyes filled with tears. "I'm sorry," she murmured, reaching across the table to pat my hand. It was such a maternal gesture that I struggled not to well up myself. She intuitively changed the subject and we chatted about the fast-approaching festive season and the Christmas play that Majbritt's class were already rehearsing for.

Finally spent, hot and sweaty, Majbritt admitted defeat and gulped her juice before slipping her trainers back on ready to go home. Annika briefly put an arm around me.

"This has been wonderful. We should do it more often, just you and me, once school is back next week."

"But surely you will be back to work too?"

"Well actually," she lowered her voice, a secretive smile spreading across her face, "I've cut my hours back to just two days a week. What we were talking about earlier – I don't want to say too much but maybe this time we might be lucky. So I need to take it easy, just in case anything … happens."

There was that lump in my throat again. A flash of memory, of a feeling; a fluttering deep within that I had felt weeks before it was finally confirmed. I could tell by the look in Annika's eye, that something was definitely 'happening'.

Lena's waxy, perfectly formed features floated on a cloud of air, tantalisingly close and yet just out of reach. I stretched out my hand to touch her, pulling against the restraints that had me pinned to my seat. Strips of heavy-duty cloth across my thighs were knotted tightly to the chair legs but when I tried to loosen them, they magically dissolved and floated away, following Lena's drifting body. I lurched forward to grab her, to catch that lily white hand which I ached to hold. Suddenly, her fist unclenched and reached out to me. Her eyes flew open, filled with panic. She called out. 'Mama! Mama!' But it was my voice I could hear; an echo of nearly eighty years ago. A panic-fuelled scream when I realised my mother wasn't climbing into the seat beside me. Her gut response was to run after the car and as I turned in my seat, frantically reaching out for the fast disappearing vision of her as we picked up speed, I saw my uncle hold her back, his face a picture of desperate sadness.

I woke, gasping for air, my throat painfully dry. And after such a vivid dream, I couldn't get back to sleep. Howard used to make me warm milk and whiskey, with a dash of vanilla and a spoon of sugar. It helped, and soon enough I was soothed back to sleep in his arms, but he's not here to do that for me anymore. I tried to rustle it up myself but the whole thing tasted bitter and it certainly didn't soothe me. I opted for tea instead and sat by the window, listening to the dawn chorus and watching the sun rise over the neighbouring beech and plane trees. The city seems so peaceful in the early hours.

I had stayed in London until I was eighteen. Then, in nineteen fifty-one, I went back to Amsterdam. Of course, I knew by then that my mother must be dead. I had heard nothing. The Red Cross and agencies that were set up after the war were inundated, trying to reconnect families, and children were their priority. However, they had nothing about her for me. And until I had that concrete proof, I couldn't let go of hope. Hope that I would find somebody. A cousin, an uncle, a neighbour. Anybody. But there was nobody left.

However, I did find love. I was a good looking girl, beautiful in fact. It didn't take long to find a suitor. His name was Frederik. He was my first love. But not my first husband. I did love him though, so much. A little older than me, he was kind and handsome. Wise yet funny. Yes, it was definitely love, not just sex. But he wasn't the marrying type. He needed to roam. He had seen things that he couldn't forget, that made him restless. So off he went, taking my heart with him, leaving me broken and alone once again. And *that's* when I met my first husband, Niels. Like Frederik, he was blond-haired and blue-eyed, and very charismatic. He was my rebound, I knew that right from the start but I was desperately lonely and filled with a frantic need to reconnect with the land of my birth. And they didn't come more Dutch than Niels. We were married within months of meeting and planned to live happily ever after. But the charisma soon wore off and his eye soon started to wander. I just knew I was destined to be alone despite the gold band on my finger.

"Was it *your* mother that died aged fifty-eight?" It was our first morning out alone, and Annika had chosen a park café not too far from us, set by a small boating lake. She nodded slowly at my query.

"Yes. She had breast cancer."

"I'm so sorry." I had guessed it would be that, judging by her age.

"It was really difficult. I mean, I trained to save lives and … there was nothing I could do, for my own mother. I watched her die." Her grief was still very raw and a part of me wished I hadn't intruded. "That's mainly the reason why I left my job. I

24

told everybody it was to spend more time raising Majbritt , which is partly true but reality is, I lost faith in myself for quite a while. My ability as a doctor. My faith in medicine. My foolish belief that I could work miracles and yet, when I needed to work a miracle the most, I couldn't do it. That … *thing* … had me beaten. Sometimes there is no cure and that's quite a bitter pill to swallow. Excuse the boring English clichés. You can tell I learnt most of my English from the television!" We laughed lightly together then fell into that companionable silence we had discovered. I stared out of the window across the park, watching star-shaped, burnt orange and yellow leaves float gently to the ground. There's something so restful about autumn. The change of colour, the comforting smell of coal fires in the air and the anticipation of evenings wrapped up with a cosy throw on the sofa.

   "How about your parents – do you know how they died? Or is that too personal?" Annika eyed me, gauging whether she was prying too far. She was. But not because it's private; more because I've never voiced it out loud. I wasn't sure how to. I've kept it to myself for so many years, that it almost feels unreal now. I never had that definite closure, that mourning over a body, that burial. Not like I did with Howard. I nearly had it with my father but it all happened so quickly, that I had to shelve my grief for later. And the longer I left it shelved, unvoiced, the more sacred my grief became. More personal. Maybe now *is* the time to talk about it, to undo the bubble wrap, a little at a time.

   "There was a bit of a war going on." I gave a derisive laugh. That had to be the understatement of the year! Annika didn't laugh. She watched me intently. She waited patiently, giving me time to collect my thoughts and formulate the words I struggled to voice. I continued, a little less reticent.

"I hardly noticed it; it was just something the grown-ups talked about. Incessantly. I was only seven – Majbritt's age. Imagine that. Imagine Majbritt living through that horror. It just happened one day. The evil that had been gnawing its way in, suddenly broke through. They just spilled into the streets with their shiny boots and immaculate uniforms. So tall, so clean. How could they be so clean? And so brutal. I didn't understand what was going on. I had seen pictures of him; Hitler. Smiling, holding children in his arms, being given flowers by pretty women. I thought he looked nice. Charming. I didn't understand what all the fuss was about. But you see, when you try to hide the truth from children, they fail to see the danger. I wish I had listened. I wish I had paid more attention to what they were saying."

"But what could you do, in reality? What could you have possibly done?"

"Begged my parents to leave sooner. To not be brave, stoic. To not stand their ground. But they were so proud. So determined to carry on as normal. I mean, this was before it all really escalated, in Amsterdam, anyway. You see, they had heard things that should've made them worry. Made them run. I would rather be a coward and have my parents with me for a lot longer. Instead, I saw my father shot in the head and before I had a chance to even process that properly, I was put in a car and whisked away to another country. I barely said goodbye! I was in shock. I wish I had clung to my mother a little longer. Kissed her a little harder. Said '*I love you*' a little louder. I will never know if she heard me, if she heard the last words I ever said to her."

I looked up to see tears trickling freely down Annika's face. She held a protective hand across her stomach.

"Oh, I'm sorry! Annika, are you okay?" I nodded to her stomach.

"Yes, yes, I'm fine. I'm just very emotional at the moment."

"Is there … any development?"

She shrugged, biting down a smile through her tears.

"I'm not thinking about it. Not yet. It's too soon." We nodded simultaneously, then laughed. She reached across to touch my hand. "But your story is so unbelievably sad. I cannot begin to imagine having to do that to save Majbritt. What a brave, brave woman your mother was!"

There was that tight pain in my throat again. I eyed Annika's tears with envy. After so many years of keeping everything in check, I know that if I gave in to tears now, I would never stop. Too much heartache, too much anguish, has been kept under wraps for that very reason. '*Never look back*,' is what Howard had said. '*Don't dwell on the past, for it will destroy your future.*' I still think he was right but a little voice keeps nagging at me lately. It's time to look back, to put my grief to bed and come to terms with the past instead of hide from it. Face it, not fear it. But I'm not sure I have the strength to face everything. Everyone. Some things have been put off for so long that I am scared of what I might find.

"There was a knock at the door one day," I paused, not sure whether I wanted to finish the sentence I had just started. Annika watched me from across the table, her refreshed coffee cup cradled in her hands.

"When was this?"

"Oh, a long time ago. A lifetime ago. Niels had just left – well, I sent him packing actually. I knew it was a mistake, almost as soon as we had married but I needed a husband. I needed to belong somewhere. His family saw me as a harlot; all I wanted was to be loved. I knew, from the onset, he wasn't a faithful man. I even saw her once, hanging around outside the apartment, skulking in the shadows, waiting for him. Now, *she* was a harlot if ever I saw one!"

Annika watched me as my mind replayed that scene, that moment when I knew I could take no more of his nonsense.

"So, who was it – the knock at the door?"

"Well, at first I thought it was another one of his women. I half expected her to say she was pregnant with his baby. But she just stared at me. She seemed nervous. She said, *'Are you Kristabel Ruebenstein?'* My heart fell into my boots at the sound of my maiden name. I just nodded, my body started to tremble and then properly shake. I could hardly control myself. *'I am Sara Ephraim',* she said. Well, it meant nothing to me, of course but I could tell by looking at her and by her name that she was from the past. I knew this was an important moment but I wasn't sure how or what. My mind was racing. A distant cousin, maybe? I invited her in, I led the way through to our small living room and indicated she should be seated on the sofa. She smiled briefly although it didn't quite reach her eyes. I could see she was as shaky as I was. I guessed she was older, maybe twenty-five years older than me. It turned out she was only fourteen years older. Then, before I could take my seat opposite her she just said, *'I have a message for you. From your mother.'* "

Chapter Three

"The floor tipped up on its end and the room started to spin. Faster and faster, speeding up, until darkness took over. I came to and she was fussing over me, offering me water. Then she made tea, in my kitchen. It was all very strange, very surreal. I waited until she sat back down. It felt like an eternity."

"Where was your mother?"

I paused, reliving that heart-stopping moment.

"She was dead. You see, *that's* how Sara should have started her sentence; *'your mother's dead, I'm sorry, **and** she left a message for you.'* Instead, for those agonising few minutes, my whole world changed. I honestly thought my mother was alive somewhere. That somehow she *had* survived. But, no. She died in Belsen. It made sense. So many Dutch Jews died there. They had said to me, years before, that it was probably Belsen. I mean, the agency; the ones trying to reunite children with their families. They told me records had been destroyed and there were thousands of people missing and not accounted for. She had been in Auschwitz – my mother – with Sara, and then not long before the war ended, they were moved. My mother was sick; Sara looked after her. She sat with her as she died. By then Sara was sick too but she was younger and had more fight in her, she said. My mother was broken. She and her sister, Elise, had arrived in Auschwitz together but Elise had a young child with her – my cousin that I never met – so they were separated from my mother. She watched as they were led away. She never saw them again. Somebody told her later that they had been killed."

"You said there was a message – what was it?"

29

I sighed. "She said I wasn't the only one to escape. My cousin Ezra was sent to England shortly after me. And I needed to find him. But it had taken her nearly twenty years to find *me*. She had been searching in England for me but of course I had gone back home."

Annika gasped. "And did you find him?"

"No. I looked everywhere I could but there were no records of him. When I came back to England I took a job with the Dutch embassy, as a secretary. Nothing important but it meant I could keep my ear to the ground, and I knew people who did searches for me. But nothing. So, I eventually came to the conclusion that he didn't actually make it after all."

"Tell me about the Kindertransport."

It was Saturday and Annika was here with Majbritt, fixing lunch for me. She usually just checks in on me over the weekends and only stops if I need anything in particular. It was my one stipulation when I employed her as my daily help; weekends are for family, and she must put her family first. But today I was feeling the cold; it had crept into my bones and the ache in my joints was unbearable. So she offered to make lunch for the three of us, insisting that I stay put in my comfy chair, with a blanket tucked under my legs to keep my knees warm. She fussed so much, pleased with her efforts, that I didn't have the heart to tell her it was my wrists and elbows that ached the most.

Startled by her question, I faltered, glancing at Majbritt.

"Oh, well, I don't think…"

Annika took the hint. "Majbritt, shall we do some colouring in the kitchen?"

Majbritt pulled a face, grabbed her rag doll and sat herself on the sofa, fixing determined eyes on me.

"I don't want to! I want to listen. I got a Kinder Surprise at Sophie's birthday party. Mine was a pink motorbike. What Kinder Surprise have you got, Kristabel?"

I tried not to smile at her earnest face.

"Pink? Surely they should have known you would prefer blue? But I bet the pink bike is wonderful. You must show me sometime."

Majbritt blinked at me, not fooled by my enthusiasm. She's a sharp one for her age. Very astute. I had a flash of inspiration.

"I have something new for you to look through." That did the trick.

"What is it?" She slid off the sofa, watching my laboured efforts to untuck the blanket and get up from my chair. We walked slowly through to my bedroom. She leant against my bed, stroking the quilted, velvet bedspread, appreciating the soft texture, all the while watching my every move. Curiosity got the better of her and she joined me, peering into the cupboard I was searching through on the far side of the room. There it was, behind a neatly folded pile of summer scarves. Her eyes lit up. We perched together on the end of the bed.

"When I was a little girl, my grandmother had a button tin. It was all different colours, heavily embossed with flowers and butterflies. They were painted purple and orange, yellow, a beautiful bright pink and emerald green, with gold paint dotted along the edges of the butterfly wings. I thought it was the most beautiful thing in the world and I would spend hours sorting through it. My mother would spread a blanket on the floor in front of the window where the sun flooded in, and the smell of my grandmother's garden wafted in through the open window. Honeysuckle, jasmine, hawthorn. Such a glorious smell. And when it rained, the grass smelled like

31

warm, sweet honey. Anyway, I started to collect buttons myself when I was older. I found this tin in an antique shop, here in London, and it reminded me of my grandmother's button tin, and so it became my hobby. No two buttons are the same! See if I'm wrong. Go on, have a look."

With Majbritt happily settled on a blanket on the lounge floor, a sea of intricate treasures spread out before her and her lunch cooling in the kitchen, Annika and I sat with our lap trays to enjoy her warm, homemade quiche and salad. It was just the tonic I needed.

"I wasn't on the Kindertransport."

"Oh! I just assumed …"

"No. The plan was for all of us – my family – to leave together. But then everything changed after my father was killed. They still told me that we were going together, to escape to England. By now I knew that England was our saviour. I found out much later, that they paid a lot of money to get me out first – all that they had left. Uncle Jusef had a friend who risked his life to save me. My mother wrote a letter and put it in my little suitcase. It was for my new family, in England. I read it years later. I still have it now, in a box." I paused, watching Majbritt sort buttons into ordered piles of colour and shape. Remarkable how such a timeless game can bring such joy.

"She wrote thank you to whoever would be looking after me. She told them she would be coming to England as soon as possible, with her parents, sister and brother-in-law. She said she had to make arrangements, you see, because her sister was having a baby."

"The one who…"

"Yes. Elise. I don't even know the name of her child."

Majbritt interrupted, enthusing about her new love of buttons. Annika sat her at the table in the kitchen to eat while she busied herself making tea for us. They seemed to take an age; I was growing impatient to finish my story. Ironic, considering how many years I've kept it quietly in my head. Finally back in the lounge, a pot of tea in front of us, she was ready for me to continue.

"I did know some of the children from the Kindertransport. We lived together, six of us, in a big, cold house in Islington. Four girls and two boys. Mrs Trigg ran a guest house before the war and she took us in. The others had been there for a while by the time I arrived. She was so lovely. Her two sons were in the army, she didn't know where. Only one came home. We all helped each other get through it; the war. There was this one girl in the house – Gabrielle – *'call me Gabbi'*, she said, *'we can all be friends'*. She was the eldest, she was fifteen. She was so smiley, so kind. Her eyes radiated a warmth I missed, so I clung to her. As did all of us. She was our lynch pin. She kept us safe, kept us smiling, kept us singing. And I adored her. Even Mrs Trigg adored her. She relied on her to help take care of us. Then, one night I had the most awful nightmare; my father's death replaying in my head but just before he was shot, he turned to look at his executioner – and it was *me* holding the gun. I woke up screaming, although it was a silent scream but nevertheless I was shaking and weeping. So I went to seek comfort from Gabbi. Kind, smiling Gabbi. And as I tiptoed to her room, I heard a muffled noise, like a wounded animal or a fox in season. I realised it was Gabbi, wailing her grief into her pillow. And it hit me, the measure of her braveness. She held her own pain and fear in, every day, to encourage us and

33

keep us happy. She was the strongest person I have ever met."

"What happened to her? Did you keep in touch?"

"She stayed in London after the war. She found out quite soon that she had no family to go back to. She was from Czechoslovakia. She lost everything. But it turned out well for her. She married Mrs Trigg's son – Tommy – a year after the war. He was very handsome, a hero. Who wouldn't fall in love with him? I was a bridesmaid, with the other girls, Marta and Sabina. Leon – the eldest of the two boys – was sixteen by then and he walked her down the aisle. And Gabbi wanted little Arno to be a page boy but he was twelve and insisted he was too grown up for that, so he wore a smart suit and was in charge of looking after the guests. It was a beautiful day. The happiest. And then we all rushed back to the house to prepare for the party. And what a party! All of Tommy's army friends were there, and the neighbours. They all scraped together with us to make a wonderful feast. We had a real cake. Not like the cardboard ones Mrs Trigg had always made for us on our birthdays. Real butter, real eggs. You wouldn't believe the moans of appreciation at that cake!" I laughed at the memory, catching Annika's look of wonder out of the corner of my eye. "What?"

She shrugged, smiling. "I would never have imagined any of this. Looking at you, I would never have guessed what you have lived through. You should write it down."

I shook my head. "Absolutely not! Who would want to read that anyway? It's just how it was, Annika. Life was different then. Things happened and we got on with it."

And that's what we did do. Of course, we all promised to keep in touch when the time came to leave the safety of Mrs Trigg's house – our home. We had come together in the

34

darkest of times; all lost and bewildered. It was a happy accident that we all ended up together but we became the best of friends. Gabbi was Czech, Marta had come from Germany, Sabina from Poland and the boys, Leon and Arno, were Austrian. They were brothers. Apart from Gabbi and Leon, we were all around the same age, Arno being the youngest – only six – and so we naturally turned to them as our guide. Out of all of us, Marta was the only one who returned to family. Her uncle had survived Auschwitz. They started a new life in America. For some reason, Leon had a hankering for Scotland and just before I left for Amsterdam, he and Arno headed up there to work on a farm. Which just left Sabina. She stayed with Mrs Trigg, helping her to run the guest house, alongside Gabbi and Tommy. Two years later, she too married and moved on. The last I heard from any of them was that Gabbi and Tommy moved to Cornwall, to open up a guest house there. And of course, Mrs Trigg went with them.

"So why didn't you keep in touch?" Annika broke my reflective trance. I sighed and stretched my aching knees.

"We did at first but life didn't work out well for me back in Amsterdam and I kept putting off the letter writing. And then we all moved on; lost addresses." I could tell she wasn't buying my excuses. "To be honest, I felt embarrassed. I had thought life would be happier for me; that being back in Amsterdam would bring me comfort. Being married would bring me joy. But the exact opposite happened in fact. My marriage failed. My last bit of hope was extinguished. Everything was slipping away from me. How could I write any of that to my Islington family? We had always agreed to be positive, to be strong. And I was falling apart."

"But surely, they would have been there to support you? You all went through so much together; surely they would have wanted to be there for you still? Don't you think?"

I didn't think. I didn't want to think. At the time I didn't have the strength to think. And then Howard appeared, scooped me up and did the thinking for me. Of course, now I'm wondering, if I had told him about them, would he have encouraged me to keep in contact? Would he have engineered it for us to all meet up again? Now I will never know.

"That's right, just a little closer. Good! Now, all face me - yes, yes. Little one on the end; chin up. Good, yes, good. Now: say 'cheese'."

"Cheese?" Leon retorted. "No, no, where we come from we say 'Shalom'!" And with a flourish of his hand, he encouraged us all to shout in our loudest voices, "SHALOM!"

"Hitler's dead!" Arno piped up, grinning as Leon reached forward to ruffle his hair.

"Yes, he bloody well is!" he replied in his best mock-English tone.

I stroked the photograph with my thumb, smiling at the image of us. I kept it safe in my box along with other treasured memories. Mrs Trigg had taken us to a local photographer on Holloway Road. He was running a special deal for returning soldiers to have their photos taken, either with loved ones or fellow comrades from the war. He was an old friend of hers and didn't hesitate to include us in his special deal. It was a time of celebration. The war was over. He had captured our jubilation perfectly. A few weeks later and our faces would have told a different story, as the aftermath of the war and reports of the total massacre of

36

Jews across Europe started to filter through. That's when the real heartache started. The hopes that we had clung to, however tiny, were slowly but surely quashed. Pictures of Bergen-Belsen emerged and shook the world to its very core. Auschwitz. Dachau. Neuengamme. I couldn't look. *My mother's strong; she would have found a way to survive. She'll be back for me*. I repeated those words over and over in a bid to quell my rising panic. More and more camps, more and more pictures emerged. Sobibor. Treblinka. Belzec. Buchenwald. Westerbork. The list kept growing and my faith kept slipping. The wait was agonising.

And then the news came. Auschwitz, Sobibor, Westerbork and Buchenwald systematically robbed me of my family. Every name I had submitted to the agency, every name bar two, came back to me with one of those four camps attached to them. It didn't happen all at once; no, the news trickled through slowly. One report at a time. In fact, I didn't find out about my grandparents until I returned to Amsterdam in nineteen-fifty-one. By then they had been dead for nine years. Every which way I turned, I was greeted with a finality that ripped my soul in two. I couldn't bear it. And then the day after I met Sara Ephraim, when I truly could take no more, I was sitting by the canal willing myself to slide into the cold water. Just disappear. Drift away into oblivion. Be rid of all that pain. But something was holding me back. And then there was a tap on my shoulder. I turned and looked up to see a stranger offering me his jacket to shield me against the rain.

Chapter Four

Majbritt sat as close to me as she could, her cold hand clutching my gloved one. Her eyeline followed mine, fixing her earnest gaze on Howard's name. Moments earlier, she had been dancing between the headstones, singing to herself and gleefully swishing the skirts of her favourite, purple, dressing-up princess gown. Annika had pulled her aside and there had been a kind yet firm exchange in Swedish, and Majbritt had hurried over on tiptoe to join me on the cemetery bench.

"Can he hear us?" she wondered.

I laughed lightly. "I hope so, otherwise I've just been sitting here talking to myself!"

She nodded and thought about it for a while. Then she drew in a noisy breath, leaning forward.

"Hello, Howard!" she whispered hoarsely, then sat back to wait. She turned to me and shrugged. I smiled.

"He's not going to answer you, I'm afraid, but he can hear you."

"Oh," she nodded. She deliberated for a moment then leant forward again. "I miss you Howard and I'm sad that you won't see me in the Christmas show because I will be wearing a blue dress. Your favourite colour!" She beamed at me, then cocked her head, listening intently. She gasped.

"He heard me! He said he wished he could be there." She settled back on the bench gesturing to me. "Your turn. Tell him about our trip to the theatre. I can't wait for that!"

This was a little more intrusive than I had expected. When Annika had offered to drive me, I hadn't really thought it through. Of course, Majbritt would come with us and of course, she wouldn't show the same reserve or respect of

38

privacy that an adult would. But I found it quite refreshing nevertheless.

"I used to like dressing up and dancing too when I was your age, usually in my mother's high heels." I lightly touched the silky, moire taffeta of her gown that twisted and shimmered in the dappled sunlight.

Majbritt's eyes widened. "Did you?"

I nodded. "Yes, I was going to be a ballerina. I had classes every Saturday morning. It was such hard work but I loved it."

"Why did you stop?"

I thought about it for a second. How to explain.

"There was this man, he was very nasty and he ruined the world."

Majbritt gave my simple explanation a great deal of thought. "Are you talking about Brexit? It's all Pappa talks about too."

I laughed – a little too loudly, too heartily perhaps – drawing curious glances from a couple nearby. Majbritt joined in my laughter.

"Did you hear Howard laughing too?" she asked.

"I did, I did. He would have found that hilarious!" I chuckled. Ah, the innocence of children. What would life be without it?

"Is this new?" Annika pointed to the framed group photo taking pride of place on the unit. She did a double-take and picked it up for a closer inspection. "Is that *you*?"

I nodded. It had been forgotten about long enough so I had ordered a polished silver frame online. Since my conversation with Annika the previous week, I'd felt somehow comforted by the image of us all together.

"Yes, that's me. Between Sabina and Arno. Marta's next to Sabina and that's Gabbi and Leon standing behind us."

"He's a handsome one – Leon."

I smiled. "Yes he was. I think we all had a crush on Leon. I didn't realise just how much until he kissed me goodbye. I was seventeen by then and very impressionable."

"And they went to Scotland, you say?"

"Yes, to a farm. Arno would have been sixteen when they left. Leon was twenty. Everywhere was short of labourers after the war, and our post master had a cousin who needed workers; the usual story. So off they went, in the rain. They sent a card at Christmas. Mrs Trigg cried and kept it on the mantle until Easter!"

Annika carefully replaced the photo. She smiled; a smile that told me she had something to say but wasn't sure how to broach it.

"I hope you don't mind but … I discovered there are some groups to do with the Kindertransport. There's one on Facebook. I had a look at it and I was wondering if you had ever looked for your friends on there?" She already knew the answer. I don't do Facebook or any other social media. It's just not me. I'm too old for all that nonsense. I said as much. She didn't accept that.

"Far from it, Kristabel! So many people your age are on Facebook, rediscovering old friends, keeping in touch with family. It's not just for the young." Sensing I wasn't yielding, she dropped the subject but kept glancing at the photograph as she hoovered the floor.

Two days later, she broached the subject again.

"It's coming up to the eightieth anniversary of the first Kindertransport, this December. There are quite a few events happening to celebrate it, in America and in this country. You really should take a look. Wouldn't it be wonderful if you found them in one of the groups!" Her enthusiasm was not as infectious as she'd hoped. I smiled and nodded in a vague, non-committal way. Undeterred, she persevered. "Would you like me to set up a Facebook page for you?"

"No!" I snapped, then checked myself when her eyes widened in alarm at my bluntness. "No, thank you. I really … I just don't feel happy doing that." My smile – the one that usually warns people not to pursue any further – went unnoticed. Or was it just ignored?

"Okay then," she countered, "how about if I have a look on your behalf. Ask if anybody has heard of Gabbi or Sabina. Or Marta – you said she moved to America. Maybe she will be in this group in New York. If there's a chance, wouldn't it be a wonderful time to reunite?"

I had that uneasy feeling creeping under my skin. I scratched at my hand, trying to ease it. My heart beat a little faster.

"I'm not sure, Annika. I don't like the idea of being public…"

"Oh no! Of course not!" she interrupted. "I wouldn't dream of it. I would be very discreet; as I'm sure they would be too. I would send a private message, nothing public." She flashed an encouraging smile but I saw the brief frown of consternation at my reluctance. I scratched at my hand a little more intensely.

"Do you have some cream for that eczema?" she asked lightly. I stopped scratching.

The eczema had first started shortly after I arrived in London in nineteen-forty. It didn't take long for bright red, blistered patches to appear all over my body; in particular, the back of my knees and neck, elbow joints, wrists and hands. I vaguely remember having a patch of it on the back of my knees when I was even younger but the move certainly made it flare up to an almost crippling degree. Those early days in Islington were permeated with the distinct smell of coal-tar and hours spent in the children's hospital ward being wrapped in bandages until the worst had past. And pass it did. With time. It had almost cleared up by the time I returned to Amsterdam and even though I had flare ups, particularly during stressful times, it never returned to the severity of the early forties.

"What are they doing here?" Papa whispered. He paused for a moment by the window overlooking the communal courtyard, momentarily halting the small procession behind him silently descending the stairs. The early morning stillness was broken by angry shouting. Mama joined him at the small window in the stairwell. She gasped, quickly covering her mouth.

"What do we do?"

"We proceed. It's nothing. I'm sure it's nothing." He motioned for us to bypass him and continue our descent, all the while watching the courtyard like a hawk. Jusef snatched up my hand – the one Papa had been holding. 'Keep moving', he mouthed, squeezing my hand in encouragement. My small bag was strapped across his shoulder and unhampered by any other luggage, we moved on swiftly down to the ground floor. Papa re-joined us, agilely taking the last stairs two at a time.

"Where…" I started but Mama hushed me, holding a warning finger to her mouth. Jusef bent to my level.

"We need to walk a little while and then we'll be in the car. But we do it quietly, okay?" He smiled and nodded, straightening up.

"Are they the monsters?" I whispered. Papa swung round, stopping Jusef's reply.

"No. No, they are just people, that's all. Nothing to worry about." Clearly agitated but desperately trying to disguise it, he ushered us to the far door. The main door would have led us directly into the courtyard, beyond which was the archway leading out onto the street. By taking the other door we came out at the back of the building by the little grassy play area, enabling us to walk around the block unseen by those in the courtyard. But as we passed the small side passageway that led back into the courtyard, Papa stopped. Raised voices again. Just two or three, barking orders in a language I didn't recognise. Papa was watching, peering round the corner, while the rest of us were shielded by the solid walls that housed our apartment.

"Stay out of sight, Isaak!" Mama's urgent tone fell on deaf ears. A woman's voice cried out in anguished protest and Papa hurried through the passageway in her direction. Jusef swore under his breath, taking Papa's position to surreptitiously observe what was unfolding. I crouched by his knees, also watching.

"Was ist das Problem heir?"

I heard Papa's voice but didn't understand the words. Jusef swore again, this time with more passion. A sense of disbelief at what Papa was doing. I could see three people I recognised. One was Mr Gerson, an elderly gentleman that Papa spent a lot of time with, discussing the affairs of the world. His arm was held in a vice-like grip by an angry soldier, pulling him to order. Mr Gerson's daughter was the one pleading; it was her cry that had prompted Papa into heroic action.

On hearing him, one of the five soldiers swung round, startled by the intrusion. He demanded to see papers; Papa

43

dutifully provided them all the while talking quietly, rationally, to the agitated man. He studied the papers and became quite still. Papa stopped talking. The air was heavy with tension; even I could feel it. I knew something bad was about to happen. He passed the papers to another soldier – his superior I assume – who started an angry exchange with Papa. It all happened so quickly; Papa was heatedly reasoning, the soldier angrily questioning and then from out of the shadows, another man stepped forward and shot Papa in the back of the head. He fell. And as Jusef scooped me up to run, another shot rang out and Mr Gerson also fell.

Instead of heading for the car, Jusef swerved off to the right and led us beyond the play area, crossing the back streets, down an embankment and stopped by a small clump of slender birch trees. Depositing me on the ground, checking Elise and briefly holding my distraught mother, he hurried back up the embankment. I wanted to wail out loud but I couldn't utter a sound. Elise vomited where she crouched. Mama stared blindly at the ground, tears cascading unchecked down her face. It seemed an eternity before Jusef re-emerged, telling us that the soldiers had disappeared, taking Papa's and Mr Gerson's bodies with them. He guided us speedily to the car and made a bee-line for Uncle Sander's house. We never returned home.

I watched Annika ceremoniously place a generous slice of carrot and walnut cake next to my brimming tea cup, and an equally generous chocolate muffin next to her coffee. I tried not to grin.

"What are we celebrating?"

She gave me a quizzical smile, placing the tray by the side of her chair.

"Do we need to have a reason to enjoy some cake?"

"Not really, I just …" I didn't want to push the issue but I've seen her absently rub the side of her stomach on a couple of occasions now. "I just don't think I have ever eaten as much cake or as many biscuits since I met you!"

She laughed. "Ah, then you haven't met a Swede before! It's tradition. Cake and coffee. It's how we roll."

I still have no idea where she puts it; she's stick thin. Although lately, she has filled out a little. I wonder.

"But having said that, I do have some news for you. I wanted to tell you yesterday but Majbritt was there, so," she stirred her coffee, assessing me. "Now don't worry, I was discreet."

"What with?"

"I sent a message to that group I mentioned." She glanced round the quiet café. "And I've had a reply!"

"Who from?" I nearly choked on my words, my throat suddenly very dry.

"Marta!"

Just hearing her name brought a tight lump to my throat. I clutched my hands together, fiddling with my wedding ring, waiting for Annika to elaborate.

"She lives in New York. That's all I know for now. She asked for an email address for you and gave me hers. She said she would write straight away, and she was delighted to hear from us – I said I was helping you to trace the old 'gang'." Annika did air-quotes when she said 'gang'. It took a moment for it all to register.

"So, any news on Gabbi? Leon?" I watched her shake her head with regret. I wasn't really expecting to hear from them; Gabbi would be ninety-three by now, and Leon eighty-eight.

There's still a chance I suppose but getting slimmer by the day.

"Do you have an email account?"

I laughed abruptly. "Of course I do. Do I know how to use it? Not really. I've mastered online shopping but that's about it, I'm afraid."

"That's okay. If you haven't used it for a while, you'll need me to talk you through it; it's all changed recently." She watched me for a moment. "How do you feel?"

"I'm not sure. Uneasy. Surprised. Excited. A strange kind of excitement, almost childlike." It had certainly taken me by surprise. I had butterflies in the pit of my stomach and a curious urge to laugh. I suddenly remembered the excitement I used to feel on the eve of my birthday. Not for the first year after I'd arrived in London but after that, yes. Mrs Trigg made sure our birthdays were a special occasion. We didn't have much money, and even less food but we did have imagination. And we all became masters at recycling; kings of inventive gifts. A doll cut out from old card, with scraps of wool for hair and a dress made from a threadbare pillowcase. Her face had been drawn on with a combination of paint and ink. She had a crooked smile, uneven eyes and scarily large eyelashes, like squashed spiders, but I loved her nevertheless. Fingerless gloves made from old socks. Embroidered lavender cushions, also made from old socks. A collection of tatty puppets for a puppet show, made from – you guessed it – old socks. When I say, 'old', they had either been handed down and outgrown, or darned to within an inch of their existence, before they could be classed as no longer fit for purpose. And with six pairs of growing feet, we worked our way through a fair few pairs of socks during the war years.

Sabina and I spent hours crafting chess pieces from candle stumps and dead matches for one of Leon's presents. He adored playing chess and insisted on teaching all of us – on the proviso that he always won, of course. And then the party games we played; Mrs Trigg was a great advocate of party games. Musical chairs, with the music provided by each of us in turn on the piano. Pass the parcel, with half a dozen 'promise' cards as gifts. '*I promise you a picnic at Alexandra Palace*', '*A day at the seaside*', '*A cheese and lettuce sandwich with real butter*'. The list of promises grew with each of our birthdays but do you know, as soon as the war was over and rationing less severe, Mrs Trigg made good on all of her promises. Except Marta missed out on the day at the seaside. She'd already left for America. The rest of us caught a train to Margate for the trip of a life-time.

I'd never seen the sea before. The beach was packed, absolutely heaving. Gabbi was married by then so Tommy acted as our protector and guide; not that we felt we needed much protecting as we were all teenagers. I had just turned sixteen, a few months after Sabina. He said that's exactly why we *did* need protecting. He wasn't wrong. It was a great time to be alive, despite all the tragedy of the darkest days. We were growing into young women surrounded by young men – heroes – returned from the war and getting used to civilian life again. That was the day, at Margate, that Sabina and I realised how easy it was to turn a boy's head; bright red lipstick and a pretty smile did the trick. We had ice-creams bought for us. Fish and chips. They even wanted to take us for a drink at the nearby pub – that's when Tommy stepped in and sent them packing. It was fun though; they meant no harm by it. And we did look pretty. Even Leon wolf-whistled – and then he laughed, of course.

"Sorry to disturb you Kristabel; I know you were going to take a nap but I had to tell you – I've had two emails!"

We'd only been back from the café for twenty minutes and, overcome with tiredness and an ache in my bones, I'd admitted defeat and taken myself to bed. Pulling the dressing gown belt a little tighter, I beckoned Annika in. She was clutching her laptop, an expectant grin on her face.

"As I didn't know your email, I gave Marta mine. And she must have passed it on to Sabina."

"Sabina?"

"Yes," she nodded, opening her laptop and logging into her emails. "I haven't read them, obviously, but they both arrived this morning."

I sat next to her at the kitchen table, a little shaky. My mind was racing and I had this overwhelming surge of relief. I would have been devastated if Sabina had died, just as I was picking up the courage to contact her again after so many years. Sixty-four years to be precise. Just after I had married Niels. I wrote and told Sabina that I was married and she'd been surprised. She'd expected me to marry Frederik; she wanted to know what had happened and how come I had married somebody else so soon? You see, I had in my blissfully euphoric state, flooded her with letters about my wonderful Frederik and our wonderful, bohemian life in Amsterdam. She and I used to share secrets when we were growing up; nothing shocking, just the usual girlie stuff. Crushes on boys; our dreams for the future. Anything to take our minds off the devastation left by war. So naturally, I told her all about Frederik and our great love affair. And I do understand why she was surprised. Disappointed, maybe? She'd sounded it. So how could I write back and tell her that I

48

had been desperately sad and thrown myself at the next boy who came along, because he reminded me of Frederik. And more importantly, how I *had* to marry Niels because he had got me pregnant. It was a total disaster, I knew it, but how could I tell her that?

Chapter Five

I could hear the smile in Marta's voice as I read her email. She was delighted to finally get contact with me, she had thought about me so often over the years. She went on to tell me about her life in New York where she's lived since nineteen forty-seven. Married, five children, eleven grandchildren and three great-grandchildren. Annika was reading over my shoulder, smiling with me. We simultaneously exclaimed a sad *'oh'* as we read about Gabbi's death seven years previously, and more upsetting, Arno's death in nineteen-eighty-one.

"He was only forty-two!"

"Oh look; cancer," I pointed at the screen. "Poor Leon, he must have been distraught."

We read on again in silence.

"Aha, look! She's on the committee organising something for the celebrations in December. What did I say? I told you somebody would be involved in it, didn't I!" Annika's triumphant smile froze and she patted my arm. "Tea?"

I couldn't shake the vision of little Arno, ravaged by cancer at such a young age. Did he marry? Did he have a good life? Marta had said nothing of that; only that she was sorry not to make the funeral. Had Leon been with him? In my head, they're still teenagers, off to seek adventures in Scotland. Did they find them?

I opened the next email. It was so stark in comparison.

'Krista Bella Bella! Where in the world are you? PLEASE get in touch! You have to come and visit me, I have waited forever for news of you!'

Bless Sabina, she always had a way of making me smile. It was Leon that had instigated my nick name – in an Italian accent – which was then shortened to Bella, and Sabina had carried it on for the few years that we had contact after I'd left England.

I stared at the phone number at the bottom of the email. What would I say? *'Oh, hello, long time no see!'* No, I couldn't do that. It's just not me. I'm not gushy like that. I'm not comfortable to just jump in where we left off. Not now, not after so long.

"Just email her back. It's that simple!"

"But what do I say after all this time?"

"You don't have to say anything really. Just let her know where you are and arrange to meet up. That's what she wants to do. And you really should, Kristabel. Think about how she is feeling too. No?" Annika stood with her hand on the back of my chair, eyebrows raised in determination. I can see where Majbritt gets it from; she's not going to take no for an answer.

"But I can't remember how to use my email account."

"That's fine; Use my account for now. I'll help you." And she did. Within minutes I had emailed Sabina with an equally short, equally bright email. She replied instantly.

'You're in London? I'm in Betchworth, Surrey. Come down tomorrow!'

I laughed in stunned surprise.

"See how easy that was? I told you. I'll drive you tomorrow."

And so it was settled. Without much input from me. Annika would drive me to Sabina's. She'd been invited along too, with Majbritt. Sabina's daughter and great-granddaughter would also be there.

I didn't sleep much. Too many memories, and thoughts of Arno and Gabbi, hijacked my rest. Too many regrets. *'Never have regrets'*, Howard had always said. But my regrets are fast overtaking my mind, swamping it with unanswered questions; of doubt, of panic, of time running out before I can change things.

"Oh Bella! I can't believe it's really you!" Sabina exclaimed. We fell into each other's arms and she squeezed the breath out of me. We studied each other, laughing, and I struggled not to join in with her tears.

Her home is beautiful; exactly how I imagined it would be. A pretty, thatched cottage with a pretty garden surrounding it. Inside, everything's floral and quaint. I felt like I had walked onto the set of a Miss Marple film. You know, with that wonderful Joan Hickson. Beamed ceilings, leaded windows, heavy curtains, a well-stocked hearth with an overflowing log basket next to it. Two cats curled up on windowsills and an obedient, aging, golden retriever, sprawled in front of the fire. The smell of freshly baked cake filled the cottage. It couldn't be more quintessentially English. Which, considering Sabina's husband is also a Polish refugee, I found highly amusing. And yet, deeply endearing. She used to dream of marrying the perfect English gent and live happily ever after in the countryside, yet fell in love with a painfully shy Polish lad, five years after the war. He was living only a few streets down from us in Islington but we'd never met until the night when she and I were allowed to go to our first dance, accompanied by Gabbi and Tommy. And there he was; Filip Kosinski. Another orphan finding his feet. They clicked instantly; it was so beautiful to witness. And I was so jealous. Everybody used to tell me I was the pretty one but I didn't believe them. Gabbi found love. Sabina found love. Leon had gone. So I think that's why I went on and on about Frederik;

about how perfect it was. I mean, it *was*, but clearly not perfect enough for him to want to stay. Or to take me with him.

Sabina didn't stop talking. Photo albums were surrounding us on the sofa and the ginger cat had made himself perfectly comfortable on my lap. It had taken a few minutes of circling and kneading but once settled, he had no intention of budging. Once the catch-up of who's who in her family was over, we started to reminisce about our teens. And once we started with the *'oh, and do you remember …'* we couldn't stop. We giggled like fifteen-year-olds, laughing all the more when Annika and Sabina's daughter, Zofia, poked their heads round the door from the other room to see what all the merriment was about.

Sabina glanced at her watch, and again five minutes later. She smiled.

"I have a surprise. Are you okay to do a Skype chat?"

I nodded, although not entirely comfortable with being caught on the hop. She bustled about getting a laptop positioned on the coffee table in front of us, brushing aside a pile of magazines and a couple of the photo albums. Patting down her hair – which I mimicked – she smiled expectantly at the screen. And there he was – Leon. Beaming. A smile so wide it reached his ears. My heart jumped a beat.

"Bella Bella! My God, woman, you haven't changed one bit! Where have you been hiding all of my life?"

I blinked, determined not to cry, holding a hand to my trembling mouth. Older, yes, but other than that, he hadn't changed. Still with that smile that lights up the room, that charms birds from the tree. That broke a dozen hearts along the way.

"Leon! How wonderful to see you!" I wanted to touch the screen, it was such a bizarre feeling; seeing him and yet, not being able to hug him. "I'm so sorry to hear about Arno." I hated saying it but I couldn't not. It's all I had been thinking about all night. He inclined his head, his smile dropping just a little.

"Yes. I still miss him. His son is the spitting image of him, which is great but also very surreal sometimes."

He has a son! The relief washed over me.

"And you? Children? Grandchildren?"

He nodded. "Yes to both of those! Two wives, four children, five grandchildren."

We chatted for a while longer; well, I laughed and listened more than chatted. We promised to meet up once the weather gets warmer in the new year. And then he was gone.

"Two wives?"

Sabina nodded, pulling a face. "He had a bit of a tough time. Drank too much. I think at first it was a way of forgetting about his family, everything he'd lost. Both he and Arno. And then it just became a habit which he really struggled to break. His first wife left. She didn't understand, I think. So he moved in with Arno and his wife, Fiona. Fiona's lovely, a real down to earth kind of woman. Born and bred in the Highlands. Nothing fazes her. She helped them through the worst of it. And then she nursed Arno through his cancer. It broke her heart but she kept going. The trouble with men is, they are so reluctant to talk about how they feel. Especially Leon. He's too busy being charming! Eventually he met Janet and she brought back the Leon we knew and loved so well. Yes, she's been perfect for him. Lovely!"

Zofia brought through some more tea and cake and we settled back again. Sabina eyed me for a while. I could tell what she was thinking.

"I've done all the talking. How about you? No children then?"

I didn't answer, I just gave a negative smile hoping that would suffice. It didn't.

"I don't understand, Bella. Why did you just disappear like that? We all tried to find you. We all kept in touch; met up when we could. And every time we did, there was a big hole. Somebody missing. I don't understand what happened. You were my best friend and you just deserted me."

"I didn't desert you!" Although I did. I could see that. "Things didn't work out for me. It was a disaster going back home; a complete disaster. My husband was an alcoholic too, although he didn't have a reason to drink. You know, his family survived the war. Yes, it was tough but they were Dutch Christians, not Jews. He was just … a pig. A real pig. Unfaithful, cruel, violent."

"Did he hit you?"

"Only when he was drunk. I wasn't a very good wife for him. I shouted back. I threw his drink away. I locked him out when he was so, so drunk. Not because I was being mean but because I feared him when he was like that. I had nowhere else to go. He had his mother. So he would either pass out on our steps or pass out in her kitchen. And then, there were the other women."

"I'm so sorry."

"It's okay. It's in the past. But you see, I was juggling a job, a home, a drunk, and trying to stay safe. It wasn't easy and I wasn't proud of it. How could I tell you this?"

Sabina moved closer and put her arms around me, drawing me in to rest on her shoulder. Such a maternal act. I could feel myself caving, wanting to talk. But I couldn't tell her everything. Not now. Not after all this time.

"You came back though; to London. Why not contact me then?"

"I was completely broken when I came back here. And it took a while to rebuild. I didn't want anybody who knew me to see me like that. Do you see? To rebuild me, I had to reinvent me, and I couldn't do that if I had people around who knew me before." I couldn't look at her. I knew her sympathy would undo me. "And then, I genuinely didn't know how to find any of you. Honestly. I had lost my belongings, my letters, my diaries."

"Lost?"

No, not lost. When my mother-in-law realised I had a new man in my life and had no intention of repairing my marriage to her drunken son, she let herself into my flat – obviously she still had a spare key – and trashed it. She took all of my belongings and threw them away somewhere, or burnt them, I don't know. She ripped up my clothes. She ripped up my magazines. She tipped cooking oil and vinegar on my bed, and smeared my lipstick all over the windows. She was more insane that her son, and she was sober! I said nothing. I did nothing. I couldn't cause a fuss. I just cleaned up the damage and acted like nothing had happened. She spat at me once, in the street. Her neighbours saw. They said nothing either. They just watched.

"Yes, lost. In the chaos, I suppose." I let out a deep sigh. "But I'm here now."

"Yes, you are! I wish you could stay; are you sure you won't?" she pleaded. "Filip will be sorry he missed you. I can't believe the one time he goes on a golfing weekend with our son-in-law, you appear!"

"I'll come back. And you come to town – you must! Let's make it a regular thing." I didn't want the day to end; I didn't want to say goodbye. I had a deep yearning for what I'd missed so desperately over the years.

Majbritt fell asleep almost as soon as she was strapped into her car seat, totally exhausted from her day of playing with Hanna. It didn't take long for me to nod off too and I awoke with a start when we arrived back home just over an hour later.

"Would you like me to make you something to eat?" Annika whispered as I opened the front door. Majbritt was a dead weight across her shoulder.

"No, no, I'm fine thank you. I've eaten so much today with all those sandwiches and cakes. If I'm hungry, I'll just heat up some soup."

"Are you sure?"

"I'm sure. And thank you for today, Annika. You were right. It *was* easy."

She smiled and nodded, whispering *"goodnight"* and watched me walk up the stairs before shutting the door of her apartment.

I sat for an age by the window, watching the traffic wind its way home, tail lights glinting like jewels in the drizzly dusk. There had been so much to take in today and I had nobody to talk it through with. I wouldn't want to burden Annika and besides, she wouldn't understand. She grew up in a different world. I'm not even sure Howard would have understood how I'm feeling. Yes, we're of the same generation but again, grew up in different worlds. Being wrenched from my family and thrown together with others also wrenched from their families, created such a bond that is life-long. Even if we don't see each other. That was made so clear to me today by Sabina and dear Leon. And the email from Marta had been one of such genuine joy. How could I have ignored them for so long? Put them on the back burner, until I was ready to face the truth. I'm still not facing the truth. Not really. I just feel that I have been playing at life. Playing at being an adult. Others do it so well; they breeze through life and take on maturity and adulthood in their comfortable stride, whereas I just feel like a phoney grown-up.

I should've stood up for myself more; against Niels, against his tyrannical mother. I just accepted it. Is that what my family did in the end – just accepted it? Being humiliated. Being degraded. Being tortured. Rounded up like cattle and slaughtered. And the world watched on. Is that what happened? Or did any of them fight the injustice? My father did and look what happened. What must my mother have gone through after that? She knew that to stand up for herself would mean risking her life. And she had to survive, for me, but she must have known in the end that she would die. That would have tormented her.

My Islington family taught me valuable lessons of trust and belonging. We trusted each other with our deepest, most frightening fears. We didn't voice them but we all felt them. The fear of losing our parents. The fear of not belonging anywhere. Of being rejected once the war and all its horrors had passed. We would be left alone to face the world. But we had each other. And we had Mrs Trigg. Valiant Mrs Trigg who protected us against the taunts and jibes, and the prejudice that comes with ignorance and fear.

I picked up the phone. "Sabina, it's me. I just wanted to thank you for such a wonderful day. And to say, I am so desperately sorry that it's taken so long. I never forgot you. Any of you. And I promise, one day I will tell you everything. Soon."

"We never forgot you either, Bella. Welcome back."

"I'm really sorry to trouble you on a Sunday," I said again, trying to take in everything Annika was showing me on the screen. She'd had another email from Marta and when she came up to show it to me, took the opportunity to get me up and running with my own emails.

"Not at all. It's all very straightforward really; it's just a case of knowing which keys to press. And with your touch screen, it makes it so much easier for you," she said. I wasn't so sure about that but I nodded in agreement anyway. I glanced round the study.

"Where's Majbritt?"

"She went to the bathroom." Annika paused and tilted her head to listen. "She's been a while, hasn't she?" She stood up. "Majbritt? Everything okay?"

"Yes, Mamma!"

We both smiled and returned our attention to the computer. A few moments later, Annika looked up again and frowned. I sensed it at the same time as her; the apartment was eerily quiet. We went in search of her. The bathroom door was ajar – no sign of Majbritt. Not in the kitchen either. Annika called again, louder.

"I'm in here!" Majbritt's happy voice was coming from my bedroom. Annika pushed the door open and there she was on the far side of the room, sitting cross legged on the floor. I froze to the spot. The cupboard door was open. The button box was by her side, and strewn across the floor in front of her, a dozen photos, folded letters, more letters bundled with elastic bands, infantile hand-drawn cards and a small frame with dried, pressed flowers in. My beloved tatty rabbit lay across her thigh and she was clutching some photos in her hand. The lid and a half-empty box had been carelessly pushed to the side. Majbritt looked up at us.

"Kristabel, is this you with a baby?"

Annika, seeing my stricken face, acted quickly. "Majbritt, these are not yours. Stand up please and give me those pho…" Her gently firm voice tailed off as she looked at what Majbritt handed her. She turned to me. "This … this baby isn't …" She quickly flicked through the handful and stole a look at more spread out at her feet.

"It's Kristabel, looking pretty, with a little boy!" Majbritt told her, pointing at the floor. Annika's eyes flew up to mine, a mix of confusion and shock assessing me. That look broke my trance.

"What are you doing in here?" I snapped. Majbritt jumped and side-stepped to clutch at Annika's leg. "How dare you look through my things!"

"Okay, I'm sure she meant no harm," Annika started, resting a protective hand on the side of Majbritt's head.

"Don't be ridiculous! Of course she meant it! Look at it all! That's *my* box, *my* private things. *My* private cupboard!"

Annika held a hand up to placate me. "Kristabel, please," she nodded at Majbritt.

"No! She is always here, poking her nose into my things. Get out! Both of you! Just leave. Now!"

Annika scooped Majbritt up, cocooning her against her chest. Majbritt burst into noisy tears.

"I'm sorry, Mamma, I didn't mean it!"

I didn't bother to see them out; they left quick enough without my help. How could she? That child is always meddling with my things. Always.

I sat heavily on the edge of the bed, reached down and picked up my rabbit. Steeling myself, I looked at the haphazard collection of aging photos that had been boxed away for a lifetime; images of a much younger me, cradling the most precious gift, the most perfect creation, who grew up to completely break my heart.

Chapter Six

It didn't take long for me to calm down once they'd left and then I spent the next few hours fretting about what I'd done, how I'd reacted. Once I was thinking clearly, more rationally, I could see what had happened. Majbritt, bored with watching us fiddle about with emails, had wandered off in search of my button tin. She had seen where I kept it; I had invited her into my bedroom before to fetch it, so in her eyes, she was doing nothing wrong. And of course, I had been showing her old photos – my wedding ones and the one of my family – and she had seen the most recent one of us at the end of the war, which I had told her I had only just found again after so many years. So, she probably thought she was doing me a favour, trying to find 'lost' things for me.

My anger at her quickly turned into anger at myself. I don't like myself at the best of times. I don't mean superficially. I look in the mirror and yes, I'm not happy about the grey hair, not happy about the wrinkles but apart from that I still look alright. I have nice clothes, I have good posture despite the arthritis but I refuse to double up, hunch over from the pain. I won't allow that to happen. But deep down, I really do not like myself. For so many reasons. So I don't dwell on it. I ignore it and live on.

It had gone seven in the evening and I knew Majbritt would be getting ready for bed. I couldn't let her go to sleep without resolving it. I hated the thought of that. Initially, I had been irritated by her, resenting her intrusion into my life, but she had unlocked something within me, and it bothered me a great deal that I had upset her. But what could I do?

"Good evening, Jan. Has … is Majbritt still up?"

Jan's reserved smile told me he was well aware of what had happened earlier. Annika appeared from behind him.

"She's in bed, Kristabel." She barely looked at me.

"Annika, please; I need to apologise to her."

"But she's in bed," she reiterated.

"Maybe Kristabel could come in and just say goodnight to her," Jan countered, holding the door wide to invite me in. "I'm just about to go and say goodnight to her myself," he smiled, leading the way. Annika followed behind, defensively clutching a storybook to her chest. Majbritt had heard us and was sitting up in bed, surrounded by a sea of teddies and soft toys. Her worried face twisted my stomach. She looked to Annika for reassurance.

"May I?" I pointed to her bed; she nodded. I perched on the edge, feeling wretched. I sometimes forget how young she is. She has such an old head on young shoulders, it's easily done. But seeing her in bed, in her pastel pink and pale blue haven that smells of baby talc and soap, I was sharply reminded of what a tender age she's at. And despite her apparent wisdom, she is still a child, living in a safe bubble, protected from the cruelties of the world.

"I am so sorry, Majbritt. I should not have shouted at you. It was very wrong of me. But you took me by surprise, you see."

She watched me with earnest eyes. "Don't you like the photos? Is that why they were hidden?"

"I suppose so, yes." I could see she was waiting for me to say more. "They make me sad. And nobody wants sad photos on display, do they?"

She shook her head. "But who was the boy with you in all the photos? Is he dead? Is it Howard?" I could see her mind was racing.

"No, not Howard. Because Howard was older than me, remember?" I tried to brush aside her question but, Majbritt being Majbritt, wasn't going to let it lie.

"Then who was he?"

I sighed, looking up at Annika and Jan's expectant faces, as eager to find out the truth as their daughter.

"He was my son."

"*Was*?" Annika breathed. I responded with a weak smile. "*Is*" I corrected.

"Why does it make you sad?" Majbritt persisted.

"Because he was very naughty. He did naughty things. Bad things. But I don't want you to worry about that now; you need to go to sleep. You've got school in the morning. We can talk about this another time. Yes?"

"Yes," she nodded, lying back down, then added, "I'm naughty sometimes. I do naughty things too but it's only because I want Mamma's attention."

"I'll make some coffee," Jan said in a hushed voice, breaking the uncomfortable silence that followed Majbritt's innocent remark. We each kissed Majbritt on the cheek and quietly left the room. As soon as we were out of earshot, I apologised to Annika for my earlier behaviour.

"I'm sorry too. I shouldn't have looked at your private photos but for one awful moment, I thought Majbritt had found photos of your dead baby."

"Oh goodness, no! I think that's a hideous tradition; I could never do that. Even if it had been an option, I would have said no." I shuddered at the thought.

"Dead baby?" Jan frowned. Annika quickly explained about Lena. I couldn't bear the sadness in his eyes when he looked at me. He ushered us to the kitchen table where he'd placed a pot of coffee and a smaller pot of tea, alongside a plate of cinnamon buns and biscuits. Tea lights flickered in clear jars on the wide windowsill and a brass side light threw a comforting amber glow across the room. I love their kitchen; there's something so homely, so familiar about it. And it always smells of spices. Nutmeg, cinnamon and cloves fill the air, mingling with the sweet smell of apple. Annika busied herself filling our cups and offering me something from the plate. When Jan saw the small pile of photos I placed in front of me, he flicked the overhead pendant light on, illuminating the table.

"This is my son, Rueben." I spread the images across the table like a pack of cards, waiting for their response. Annika picked them up individually, silently studying them before passing them on to Jan.

"Rueben? As in Ruebenstein?"

I nodded. "Yes. I wanted to name him Isaak, but I knew that every time I'd say his name, I would hear an echo of my mother calling my father. And that would break my heart. So I opted for Rueben."

"But you named your daughter Lena."

"Yes," I sighed deeply, "I didn't know then … I mean, I was still holding a hope that my mother was alive somewhere. And of course, four years later, I found out she was dead. An irrational part of me was convinced I had tempted fate by naming my dead baby after her."

"But that's ridiculous!" Annika interjected.

"I know that now but you must understand, it was a ridiculous, irrational time. I barely coped with it and my mind tormented me. So much."

They sat in respectful silence, listening, allowing me to air my grief. Jan slid the photos back towards me.

"So what happened? I mean, where is he now? In London?"

"He was, yes. But he didn't like Howard. He blamed Howard for ... well, for everything, really. He was a very difficult teenager. I understand it wasn't easy for him, being uprooted and moved to a different country. He was only twelve when we came here with Howard. He struggled to fit in. He got teased because of his accent and his looks. He was very handsome, very athletic, with blue eyes and blond hair. He got into fights because he was mistaken for being German, and the war was still very fresh in the minds of many so you can imagine how the English felt about Germans. But ..."

"But?"

"He found a new friend. And it destroyed him, destroyed us. It turned him into a criminal, a thief. It made him aggressive, unforgivably rude; such bouts of violence. He reminded me so much of his father and I struggled to cope with that. We argued all the time. I was scared for him. I was hurt how he treated Howard. Howard did everything to give us a new life. He brought us over here, provided us with a lovely home, a safe haven. But Rueben just threw it all in our faces." I stopped short, realising my voice was rising. Even now, even after all this time, I still see red when I think about it.

"His friend – was it drugs?" Jan is very astute.

"Yes. Anything and everything. He quickly became addicted to heroin but tried anything. Anything he could get his hands on to escape reality."

"Didn't you get help for him?" Annika pitched in. My laugh was a little too derisive, I realise that but her question irritated me.

"This was a long time ago, Annika. Nowadays yes, they're dishing out support hand over fist but back then, we just had to cope. It was a new problem; nobody really understood it then. And yes, we tried but to be helped, you have to *want* help, and he didn't. He didn't want anything from us. He ran away. We were frantic; Howard more than me, to be honest. By then, I was completely drained by it all. It made me ill. Well, Howard walked the streets for days, looking for him. He found him in the end, sleeping rough with a couple of men. Howard said they looked so dishevelled and had probably been on the streets for some time. He offered to buy them breakfast, then asked Rueben to come back with him. All Rueben could say was, *'you're not my dad. You can't tell me what to do.'* Howard did the only thing he could; he went to the police and they picked him up and brought him home. He was so angry with me, so angry. But at least he was safe. I woke up the next morning and he was gone again. I got a phone-call three days later from Niels, telling me Rueben had gone back to live with him. Then he condemned me for the state of him; said I had neglected our son. Neglected! I couldn't believe it! So I hung up."

"Then what?"

"Then what? Well, what else could I do? I carried on with my life and he carried on with his."

I wasn't sure how to read the silence that followed. I realise there was a lot to take in and I apologised for burdening them with it. Jan shook his head, murmuring, *"don't be silly."* He regarded me for some time.

"How old is Rueben now?"

"Sixty-four."

Annika gasped. Jan patted her hand. "And how old was he when you last saw him?"

I swallowed hard. "Fifteen." This time neither of them could hide their shock. Jan shook his head slowly, grappling with the concept.

"But that's forty-nine years. How can that happen?"

I didn't reply. What could I say? It just happened. He left. I picked up the pieces of my shattered world – again – and nursed my broken heart. It's an unbelievably deep hurt; being rejected in favour of the one person I was trying to protect him from. So I let time slip by unnoticed and pretended it wasn't happening. It is remarkably easily done. You keep telling yourself, *one day we'll resolve things*, but deep down you know that day will never come. Time widens the gap, strengthens the barriers and deepens the resentment until you lose sight of what was real, and only remember the hurt and bitterness.

The phone was ringing again. I could hear it; I just didn't want to answer it. I heard Annika knocking at the door a few minutes earlier. I heard her call; quietly at first, then more urgently. She wasn't going to give up. Sighing, I reached for the phone on the bedside table.

"Hello?"

"Kristabel! Are you alright? I'm outside! I've been knocking."

"Yes, yes, I'm sorry. I don't feel very well. Maybe forget today; I don't need anything. I just need to rest."

"Okay," she sounded unconvinced. "Did you sleep?"

I didn't reply. I couldn't actually bring myself to lie. Not after last night.

"Have you eaten breakfast?"

"I'm fine, thank you, Annika. I'll eat later when I feel better."

Still unconvinced, she fired a few more questions before hanging up. I sank back against the pillows. I'm sure I had slept eventually but it really didn't feel like it.

I had left Jan and Annika to mull over everything I'd divulged. The stunned silence hadn't really lifted and not knowing what else I could add, I'd awkwardly taken my leave and retreated to the dark sanctuary of my bedroom. But sleep completely eluded me. My legs ached; not with arthritis but with a restlessness I couldn't shake off. Donning my winter coat and warmeries, I took a slow walk down the street. The cold air hit me, filling my lungs with an iciness that used to excite me.

I've always loved the night air, particularly at this time of year. You can smell it – the promise of long evenings by the fire, the excitement as winter approaches, bringing with it all the festivities. Howard loved Christmas and always made a big fuss over it. Once rationing was finally over, Mrs Trigg had treated us to our first, traditionally English Christmas; complete with rich mince pies and brandy butter, plates piled high with assorted vegetables, beef sausages and turkey, all drowned in a puddle of steaming gravy. And when Howard brought us here, he made such an effort, making sure Rueben had a Christmas to remember. It was the first time I'd seen him smile in months; Howard noticed it too and felt sure he'd succeeded in winning him over. We had dared to dream that this would be our future; the three of us living happily ever after in the city that had offered me refuge twice in my young life. I honestly thought my future would be flawless; that we would grow old together, enjoying the grandchildren Rueben would provide us with. That I would be the lynchpin, the one my growing family would turn to for support and wisdom, and unconditional love. That's what I had always wanted. So badly. I wanted to be needed. To be central in a bustling family, with happiness all around. Such a simple wish, nothing extraordinary. It's what got us through the dark evenings of war. Sabina, Marta and I would huddle on the back doorstep of Mrs Trigg's bricked courtyard, watching dusk settle. The blackouts were up and the world was in darkness, holding its breath, anticipating night raids. We used to whisper our plans to each other. We can't have been more than nine or ten but even then, our young heads had determined exactly what we wanted for the future. It involved trees and gardens filled with flowers, kitchens bursting with warmth and shelves laden with food, and a house full of children. They would be well fed, well loved, and always laughing. Always safe. Always warm. And at the end of the day, we would tuck them into their soft beds and kiss them goodnight before returning downstairs to make supper for our parents – now doting grandparents — and husbands. Such simple, innocent dreams of domestic bliss that seem so dated nowadays but they got us through the most challenging times.

Sitting on the bench further down the street, I nodded a polite greeting to a couple walking hand in hand, their little spaniel dutifully leading the way. I watched their progress as they worked their way back home. They can't have been more than fifty years old. I envied what would come next. They would shut themselves in, settle down for the night, content from their busy day and eager to share news of it with each other. Maybe they'd plan the week ahead. Maybe their children would phone to check on them and wish them goodnight. Maybe they'd be planning Christmas, maybe they had grandchildren to shop for. Simple things, normal things. Sabina and Filip would by now be tucked up in their cosy cottage; I could picture it so clearly. Filip would be in the wide armchair by the lit fire, with the dog at his feet, and Sabina would be on the sofa with a throw over her legs and a cat on her lap. The ginger one with velociraptor claws, no doubt.

Spent from entertaining family – who apparently always come round for Sunday lunch – they would sit and chat amiably about nothing in particular until it was time for bed. I miss that. Just talking; no agenda, nothing really important to discuss or debate. Just idle conversation. Whenever I'm with Annika, every conversation has a purpose. I realise it's because we are getting to know one another but sometimes I would just like to enjoy a chat about nothing in particular. I miss Howard. And on evenings like this, when I need a hug and to hear his reassuring voice, I miss him the most.

Chapter Seven

There was a knock at the door again. It had been three days and yes, I know Annika's concerned about me but I just can't be doing with her well-meaning smile and probing questions. To say nothing of Majbritt. I simply can't face them.

The phone rang. Annika's number again. I had quickly learnt this week that if I don't answer and tell her I'm okay, she won't stop phoning. Or knocking.

"Hello, Annika," I started, resignation weighing heavily in my tone.

"It's Sabina. Are you going to let me in or do I need to get somebody stronger to break the door down?"

I floundered. "What?" She just tutted and hung up. My mind racing, I hurried out of bed and put on my dressing gown. Well, I say *hurried* but of course, that's an exaggeration. I felt quite light headed and unsteady on my feet. I opened the door to be greeted by Sabina's mock chastising look and Annika's overly concerned one. Behind Annika, Zofia hovered with a bunch of flowers and a pack of croissants, presumably from the nearby Sainsbury's Local. I recognised the packaging. Sabina's face quickly changed when she saw my ashen one, and taking my arm, instructed me to get back into bed. I balked at the idea of them seeing me in bed but at the same time, my legs felt like jelly. I slipped gratefully back under the duvet.

"In future, you should let Annika have a key. She's been so worried about you. Anything could've happened; you could've broken your hip and been lying here for days! Budge up." Sabina waved a hand at me to move along so she could sit next to me. I made an attempt at straightening out the duvet, expecting her to sit on the edge but instead she clambered, rather ungainly, onto the bed and propped herself up next to me and took my hand. She pulled a face and grimaced. I recognised that look.

"Dodgy knee?"

"Hip. I broke it eight years ago and had a hip replacement but it still aches, especially when the weather turns. Amazing what they can do though, with hips and knees."

Zofia offered me the flowers, asking if I'd like her to put them in water.

"We got you chrysanthemums – I remember they were your favourite, weren't they?" Sabina smiled brightly, then nodded for Zofia to leave. She went in search of Annika in the kitchen, where I could hear tea things clattering together. Sabina's smile dropped. She turned to me.

"What on earth is going on, Kristabel?" I could tell she was concerned by the use of my full name. "What's happened?"

I sighed heavily. "I can't…"

"Yes, you can. You must! You can't shut yourself away like this, scaring Annika and Jan half to death, and not talk about it! She phoned me in such a state this morning, saying she's so worried about you."

"Did she tell you?"

"Tell me what? Why don't *you* tell me."

I watched her, my heart sinking. She never had been a very good liar. She relented.

"Only that you have been carrying a very big secret for far too long and she's worried that the weight of it will break you." Yes, it sounded like something Annika would say. Part of me wished she had told her more to save me from doing so. Sabina squeezed my hand. "We went to hell and back, you and me; what could possibly be worse? We always promised to trust each other with our lives. Well, I'm here. Trust me with this."

Sabina listened patiently, intently, as I told her everything I had told Annika and Jan just days before. There wasn't a hint of the judgment I had dreaded. There was just clear-eyed understanding. Annika had quietly appeared with a tray of tea and warmed croissants, and equally quietly, disappeared again.

"Well, I think you have to try and find him. Don't you? But where would you start to look? Amsterdam, I suppose." She studied my face. "This explains so much, Bella, so much. There's no point going over it but I *wish* you had found me sooner. I *wish* I had been allowed to be there for you. Through all of it. Good and bad. But we have to focus on the now; what to do next. I mean, you *do* want to find him, I'm presuming?"

"I'm not sure what I want. I'd accepted that I wouldn't ever see him again but since Howard died, I keep having moments of sheer panic. I want to but I don't know how to. Maybe it's best to just leave it as it is."

"No! This is *your son*. Imagine if he is also thinking, *'I want to but don't know how to'*, and then you die and he is left with that racking guilt. Is that what you want?"

"Of course not!"

"Right. Well then." She put her arms around me and hugged me, patting my shoulder. "Where to start."

"Germany."

"Sorry?" For a fleeting second a look of unease crossed her face.

"He lives in Germany, Sabina. With his German wife and German children."

I looked him up once, on Eileen's Facebook. She was showing me how it worked. This must have been about ten years ago now. She left the room to make tea and I typed in his name. There were a few Heijmans but it was almost instant. There he was! Looking so much like his father. He was living in Düsseldorf with his wife, Inge. There were photos of them with children; two, as far as I could make out. And then Eileen came back into the room. I never went down that road again. I felt physically sick at the thought of it; of where he was living and who he was married to.

"But surely you can't hold it against her? She had nothing to do with the war – she's of a different generation." The four of us were eating a late lunch in the kitchen which Annika had quickly rustled up. She and Zofia had been brought up to speed by Sabina, and Annika was voicing her surprise at my feelings towards my daughter-in-law. Sabina shot me a look but it was Zofia who tried to justify how I felt.

"To be fair, Annika, you and I can't possibly imagine what it was like back then. It's easy for us to think rationally, and I agree it does seem unfair to judge somebody purely because of their nationality but I have seen it from the other prospective. My father used to shake just hearing somebody speak in German. And all the archive footage that's been shown over the years just cemented that fear for him; that vision in his head of a soldier shouting commands viciously at his mother, in a language she couldn't possibly understand. I know when Mum and Dad took us to Auschwitz, they didn't expect it to affect them to the extent that it did. I don't think he ever recovered."

I think I stopped breathing for a second. I turned to Sabina.

"You went to Auschwitz?"

She nodded. "Yes. We had to. To pay our respects, to remember them. To show our children."

"Show them where their family was *slaughtered*?" My voice was barely audible. Sabina looked away. Zofia gave her a small smile.

"Have you never been then, Kristabel?" she asked.

I shook my head. I was struggling to comprehend how Sabina and Filip could have.

"Did you not think it would help you, too?"

"No," I replied forcefully. "And like your father, I too feel shaken when I hear somebody speak in German. I saw them, you see. I heard them. That angry, ugly voice was the last one my father ever heard. The difference is, Zofia, your parents can only guess at how *their* parents died, whereas I saw my father killed, in cold blood, by a German."

She had the decency to look embarrassed and quietly apologised. I looked at each of them, an anger rising within me.

"How can I accept this? I wouldn't even be able look at her. Her grandfather may well have been the last face my father saw. Or my uncles, my aunts. My cousins. I will never know for certain, but how can I take that chance?" I turned to Annika. "How can I not blame them? All of them. They knew. They knew what was going on!"

"Yes, but Inge is of a different generation. You said yourself that Rueben was picked on for just *looking* German and you thought that was unfair."

"Yes but that was different. After the war, people were very suspicious of foreigners for quite some time and I can understand that, after everything we had been through in the war. Spies everywhere. Walls have ears. It was drummed into us to be suspicious. It wasn't fair but I understood it." I paused, giving it some thought. "But I can't understand this. However unfair you think it is, it fills me with panic. If she's the same age as him …"

"What?

"Then her parents and grandparents lived through the war and all the anti-Semitism. It was drummed into them, just like being anti-German was drummed into us here. That's so hard to shake off. It is, Annika."

She gave a non-committal smile, pulling a disappointed face at her empty coffee cup and stood up to refill the kettle, offering more tea and coffee to the table. Taking the cue, Zofia changed the subject to talk about the new John Lewis Christmas advert that was the talk of the internet. Sabina smiled at me, slowly nodding. I think that was her way of saying she understood how I felt. Was it so irrational of me? Really? Once the war was over, I read so many articles about Germany, about the Hitler Youth, about their ideals. About the rise of a nation fuelled on a hatred of Jews. I read, I listened, I devoured the news. Until the day came when I found out my family's fate. After that, I stopped reading, stopped listening. I couldn't bear to think about it. And Howard taught me that the anger I felt and the desperation that weighed me down was wasted emotion. It couldn't bring them back. It couldn't change what had happened. He was right, of course. So I buried it deep within me, hoping that the pain and anger would go away.

Chapter Eight

Majbritt grinned at me, wriggling back in her seat and smoothing out the skirt of her midnight blue, velvet dress. She had earlier pointed out the scattering of embroidered stars across it, each one with a tiny silver sequin in its centre. Just in case I hadn't noticed, she informed me. Her hair had been brushed smooth and swept back with a glittery Alice band. Annika stepped back from the kerb and waved as the taxi pulled away. Majbritt barely waved back; she was too excited and too busy watching which way the 'friendly driver' was taking us. Pippi Longstocking sat between us and I noticed she'd been through the wash; she was definitely less grubby, less obviously loved, than usual.

The day had finally arrived for our trip to the theatre. We had kept the outing a surprise. If Majbritt had known about it, Annika felt sure she wouldn't stop going on about it for days beforehand. For that, I was very grateful. Initially, I had extended the invite to all three of them but Annika insisted I should take Majbritt alone and she would meet us afterwards to take in the lights. As it turned out, the trip was perfectly timed and had become a bit of a re-bonding exercise after the photographs incident two weeks earlier. We had patched things up, Majbritt and I, in our own way but I did agree, this would really help to get us over it.

Traffic through the city was slow, which is always the way on a Saturday and especially during the build up to Christmas. Watching the delight on Majbritt's face as she took in all the decorations and thousands of lights strung across the streets and illuminating shop windows, was an absolute treat. And when we pulled up outside the theatre, her mouth dropped open. She turned to me, excitedly jabbing at the window.

"The Lion King! Are we going here?"

I nodded. I had chosen the Lyceum theatre for its architecture more than for the show but as it turned out, *The Lion King* is her most favourite Disney film, Annika had reliably informed me. It didn't disappoint. Majbritt jumped out of the car as soon as she was unstrapped, to hug the nearest neoclassical column – one of six – that grace the theatre entrance. Unable to, due to its sheer size and her tiny stature, she turned to hug me instead. She skipped up the few shallow steps to the entrance and stopped just inside the foyer, mesmerised. It was certainly a popular show and Majbritt wasn't alone in dressing up for the occasion. The foyer was buzzing with lively, excited chatter as children and their adults gathered. Some stood shyly, some twirled on the spot to show off their pretty dresses, and one boy would insist on running about, weaving in and out of the crowd, and launch himself into an empty space to see how far he could slide. His mother had clearly given up calling him to order; that task fell on one of the ushers, with a smile that masked a thousand other feelings, I'm sure.

"Would you like a programme, Majbritt?"

She tore her eyes from the row of velvet-soft Simbas, frowning at my question.

"It's full of pictures of the show," I explained.

"Yes please!" She returned her gaze to the soft toys, eyes wide with longing. I smiled and nodded to the young lady at the kiosk. Understanding my nod, she beamed at Majbritt.

"Which one would you like?"

Majbritt's mouth dropped open again and she spun round to me. She does do reactions rather dramatically. I tried not to laugh.

"Go on, Majbritt; tell the lady which lion you want."

79

Beyond ecstatic, she pointed to one in the middle and jigged up and down, watching it being lifted from the shelf. She clutched it to her chest.

"Thank you! Thank you!"

"Call it an early Christmas present."

The lady smiled, watching our exchange as she handed back my card.

"Aren't you lucky to have such a kind grandma!"

"She's not my grandma," Majbritt replied quickly, waving her thanks as she skipped away. I have to say, the stab of disappointment I felt was quite unexpected.

We took our seats in the stalls and I watched her stare round the auditorium, drinking it all in with a wonder that reflected in her angelic face. The highly decorated boxes with their velvet swags, the vast ceiling and the plush seats didn't go unnoticed. Majbritt pointed to the Rococo cherubs on the box just above us, then continued to point as she noticed more and more cherubs and the fantastically detailed carving that swirled across the breadth of the auditorium. Her head turned this way and that; all the while she clutched my arm as she twisted in her seat. A curious ache tightened my stomach and I almost had an urge to cry. Most unexpected. Just the sight of her eagerness with a hint of vulnerability in new surroundings, coupled with the trusting way she clung to me, really affected me. He blond hair gleamed under the lights and her clear blue eyes flashed with anticipation. She could have easily been my granddaughter. My daughter, even. Rueben had all the characteristics of Niels and I have no doubt that Lena would have had too. Maybe she would have grown to look like Annika. Maybe Rueben's daughter has. I reached out and touched Majbritt's soft hair. She turned, grinning, and settled in her seat. She nuzzled her new soft toy.

"Thank you, Kristabel."

"Do you know what, Majbritt – I think you *can* call me Grandma. If you still want to?"

She gasped with delight, nodding her head and squeezing my arm tightly. The lights dimmed and the hubbub ceased. A solitary, infantile cheer went up from somewhere in the balcony. A spotlight shone on the black stage as Rafiki started to sing, *The Circle of Life*. Another spotlight lit up one of the boxes to the left and then to the right, as characters sang from there too. The stage slowly turned orange to signify the rising sun and singing could be heard from behind. I knew what was coming next; it's why I had chosen the aisle seats in the stalls. Majbritt squeezed my hand, her whole body rigid with disbelief as a huge rhino slowly made its way through the auditorium, brushing past our seats. Majbritt instinctively reached out her hand and touched it. She didn't notice the two actors beneath the costume with their heads poking out from the top. She was completely convinced that she had just stroked a rhino. More creatures appeared, making their way up to Rafiki, and soon the stage was filled with cheetahs, zebras, giraffes and a magnificent elephant. Their voices filled the theatre, drowning out the handful of children singing along, including Majbritt. She quite literally sat on the edge of her seat for the entire performance, completely captivated.

By the time the show finished it was already dark outside and we were greeted in the foyer by Annika. Letting go of my hand, Majbritt ran to her, shouting excitedly about the show. Half of it was in Swedish but you didn't need a translator to see how much she had enjoyed it. She thrust Simba in Annika's face, demanding she smell it.

"It smells like the theatre!" she explained, smelling Simba again herself and hugging it tightly. She beamed at me. "This is the best present I have ever had!"

Taking Majbritt's hand and offering me her other arm, Annika guided us along the bustling streets to Covent Garden. A crowd had gathered in the Piazza by the gigantic Christmas tree smothered in red and white fairy lights, to watch a couple of street performers. Enthralled by their costumes, Majbritt wriggled her way to the front of the crowd, dragging an apologising Annika with her. Not as eager to watch, I slowly worked my way round the edge of the crowd until I had a good vantage point. I could see Majbritt, her face just a giant, toothy grin, watching the show with delight, taking in every detail of the juggling duo as they balanced on stilts. Music blared out from their sound equipment and she jigged along to the music, her hair swishing as she hopped from foot to foot. She clapped enthusiastically at the end – a little hampered by Simba tucked under her arm – and turned to beg Annika for coins to throw into the performer's red and gold hat. The crowd dispersed; we were reunited and ventured on into the market place.

I have always loved Christmas time at Covent Garden. Howard and I would spend hours window shopping, gift buying and tea tasting here. We'd make a day of it, with lunch in the pub and dinner in one of the many eateries, before strolling along the Strand and Leicester Square to see the lights. I never tired of it. But this was the first time I'd been here without him and I have to say, I struggled with it. I did my best to focus on Majbritt and to share in her delight at everything sparkly. We have that in common. There's something liberating about Christmas time, when you can indulge in that deep-rooted love of all things shiny and pretty, whatever age you are. It brings me comfort, it transports me back to a happy time way back in my past. Flashes of my childhood home, where candlelight always shone. Where silverware always gleamed and sparkled as the light reflected in it. The smell of polish as my mother would sit all morning, lovingly polishing her silverware, softly singing to herself. The smell of freshly ground coffee would hang in the air, mixed with the warm smell of freshly baked bread. That's the smell I awoke to each morning for the first seven years of my life. That's the smell that transports me back in an instant.

"Mamma, take a picture!" Majbritt was pointing at the enormous, silver baubles surrounded by equally enormous sprigs of mistletoe and lanterns that hung from the glass and iron, market hall roof. The simplistic, yet highly effective, decorations ran the length of the hall, casting a magical show of light that bounced off the walls. Each mistletoe berry was a bright bulb, and each bauble – a mix of plain and disco-ball effect – was filled with a tangle of bright fairy lights. The shop windows were jam packed with enticing gifts, nestled in tinsel and blankets of fake snow, and the aromas that wafted out hit us with a force. I could easily pick out spiced apple, cloves, warm cherry and spiced tea and was instinctively drawn to the welcoming bouquet of Earl Grey tea emanating from Whittard's. Majbritt made a bee-line for the *Alice in Wonderland* tea set on display, while Annika and I took a moment to sample their latest blends of tea and coffee.

Next stop was the Moomin Shop which, Annika whispered, was the main purpose of our visit. The tiny shop, filled from floor to ceiling with Scandinavian gifts, was any child's dream. It was hard to tell who was more excited. Annika's face was a picture of joy as she relived her childhood, perusing old favourite characters in the shape of cushions, soft toys, back packs, crockery and endless stationary. Giving me a conspiratorial nod, I distracted Majbritt while she hurried to the till with an armful of gifts.

We stopped for something to eat, serenaded by a string ensemble playing Strauss just outside the little café. Majbritt chatted non-stop about the show, dancing in her seat to the *Trish Trash Polka*.

"I love this music, Grandma! Do you?"

Annika's eyes widened in surprise and she turned to me, questioning. I smiled, nodding acknowledgement. She held a hand to her mouth and looked away, blinking frantically to stop tears. She reached for my hand and squeezed it. It was in that moment that it hit me how blind I had been. Christmas is difficult for me without Howard and spending time with Majbritt right now when thoughts of Rueben and Lena are so fresh – thoughts of grandchildren I haven't met – make it harder still. It just hadn't occurred to me that Annika was finding it difficult too. For the same reasons. Seeing other mums out shopping with their mothers, seeing grandchildren being spoilt by doting grandparents. Annika must be missing her mother so keenly. Had she found a mother figure in me? Is that why she took such an interest and why she was eager to encourage a relationship between Majbritt and myself? I was quite appalled at how long it had taken me to consider that. As we left the café I took the lead and offered her my arm and Majbritt my other hand.

"Let me show you two the lights on Carnaby Street before we head home." Of course what I meant was, *'let me share our old haunt with you'*. I had intended to point out where our favourite record shop had been and where we always stopped for breakfast on a Saturday morning but when we got there the moment was completely hijacked by a fantastic light tribute to Queen – or more specifically, *Bohemian Rhapsody*. Lyrics from the song were emblazoned in neon lights across the street, a line at a time. Over-tired and over-excited, Majbritt jumped up and down every few steps, demanding we read out the next line. To her absolute delight and amazement, I started to sing the lyrics, quietly at first but when Annika joined in, our volume increased. Majbritt stood still, mouth open, watching us. She clapped and did a pirouette on the spot, nearly falling into passers-by.

"How do you know the song?" she demanded. I laughed.

"It was one of my favourites, a long time ago. Before your mother was born, in fact," I said in a mock whisper. She gave a knowing nod.

"And did Howard love it too, Grandma?"

"He did."

"I thought so," she sighed. She turned to Annika, stretching her arms out. "I'm tired, Mamma."

Annika faltered. "I can't really lift you right now. Can you walk a little way?" She shot me a look. I took the hint.

"I'm tired, too. Shall we all hold hands and get a cab at the end of the road?" I encouraged. I'd seen that hint of a smile on Annika's face. I bet I'm right.

The pair of them fell asleep in the taxi home. I had a sudden maternal surge of emotion that I haven't felt in many years as I watched them sleep. It was swiftly followed by an ache of regret. I called Jan on my rarely used mobile phone, making sure he was ready to greet us at the door. Majbritt briefly opened her eyes when he lifted her out of the taxi, and smiled when I blew her a kiss. Annika hugged me, murmuring her thanks and watched me walk up the stairs and open my door before closing hers. I sat by the window for some time, deep in thought. The day had brought about such a mix of emotions; some surprising and some unwanted.

  I knocked quietly on the door. Jan answered.

  "Is everything alright, Kristabel?"

  "Yes, yes, it's fine. I have a favour to ask. I need your help to find someone."

Chapter Nine

Of course, I fretted about my decision as soon as I'd made it. Was it too rash? Christmas is looming; am I feeling too emotional and not thinking clearly? What if he doesn't want anything to do with me still, even after all this time? What if he still absolutely hates me and I have just opened myself up to more pain and hurt? These thoughts went round and round in my head; a relentless carousel of self-doubt and torment.

"I'm sure it will be fine, I'm sure he will be over the moon," Annika had said.

"This is exactly what you need! It'll be wonderful!" Sabina had said.

"I think you're taking the right course but you must be aware that it all happened a long time ago. Maybe he will find this too difficult. Maybe he won't want to deal with it. I think you should prepare yourself for that," Filip had said. Jan said nothing. Jan got busy on the internet. Jan knew what he was doing. And so I had to just wait and trust him.

"Any news?" I asked. Annika shook her head, forcing a smile. It had been four days. Surely Jan could have contacted him on Facebook by now. That would take two minutes; what was the delay?

"No, that's not the way to do it. I mean, contacting your old friends on Facebook was fine but this takes more tact. No? Jan has it all in hand, don't worry." Annika could tell that was easier said than done. She put an arm around me. "*Try* not to worry. Now, about Christmas. Do you think Sabina and Filip would like to come here for Lucia, on the thirteenth? It's nothing too grand, just a few friends for drinks and food. And Majbritt will be singing for us. What do you think?"

"Yes, I'm sure. That sounds lovely," I mumbled, my mind elsewhere.

"And Christmas Eve – that's our Christmas and we would be honoured if you share it with us. But I warn you, it'll be a full day of food and music, and sitting around talking. And no doubt, watching a Disney movie. Or two. It'd be lovely if you joined us."

I blinked, brought back to reality. She smiled expectantly, waiting for an answer.

"I would love to, thank you, Annika. And I shall phone Sabina later and ask about the thirteenth."

She smiled, pleased. "And maybe extend the invite to Zofia and her husband. That'd be lovely!"

There was a knock at the door two days later in the afternoon. Majbritt was there, Simba tucked under her arm. She looked so different in her bottle green school pinafore, with her hair scraped up into two pigtails. She was clutching a card, colourfully painted and covered in silver glitter; a big grin on a tired face.

"For you, Grandma!" she announced, offering me the card. I looked beyond her down the stairs. Annika waved, calling "I'll be up in a minute!"

Majbritt skipped in and headed straight for the lounge, scanning the room for anything new.

"Where's your tree?

"Tree?"

She settled herself on the sofa, waiting for me to join her. "It's the first of December tomorrow; you have to have a tree ready for Christmas!"

"Ah, I see. Is yours ready?"

She shook her head. "No. We are doing it tomorrow, ready for Advent on Sunday. I'm baking biscuits with Mamma tomorrow. I can bake some for you too, if you want." She smiled then looked pointedly at the card on my lap. "Read it then!"

Bits of glitter showered onto my knees when I opened it. The writing was very neatly done, with extravagant flicks and tails on each letter in an attempt to join them together. I caught my breath. She expected me to read it aloud and gestured as much with her impatient hand signals.

"To Grandma, please come to my school play next Friday. Love from Majbritt" I smiled at her, warmed by her pleased expression. She widened her eyes, waiting for a response.

"Thank you, Majbritt. I wouldn't miss it!"

She pressed her head against my arm by way of expressing her joy. I patted her leg.

"Fetch me that plastic bag over there, would you? Please."

She dutifully slid from the sofa and handed it to me. I handed it back to her.

"For you, for tomorrow. And not before!"

She opened it up and gasped, sitting cross legged on the floor to inspect it further. I had been thrilled to find it; I had no idea they made things like this. It was a Disney *Frozen* advent calendar, with a little figurine behind each door. The calendar then converted into a winter scene for the figurines. I knew she would have hours of fun playing with it; much better than chocolate, which would be eaten and forgotten in an instant. She was absolutely delighted with it, which she told me repeatedly for the next five minutes, until Annika appeared to take her back home.

"Any news?" I mouthed. She shook her head. It's what I had expected anyway but I still felt the need to ask.

The week flew by with no news from Jan but plenty of news from Sabina and Marta. Marta made up for the many miles between us by emailing every few days and Sabina made up for lost time by phoning every other day. At first, I was swept away on a wave of nostalgia and left feeling quite giddy from it but as the days past, I ran out of things to say. Nothing new to report. Old memories already revisited. Both Marta and Sabina had busy family lives and shared their offspring's news with me too, which was lovely but they're not *my* family – I've never met them – and I couldn't reciprocate with tales of my family because I have none. I got to the stage where I ignored a call from Sabina. I felt wretched afterwards but I just wasn't feeling the joy that they were. I had nothing new to bring to the group. Why would anybody want to bother with me anyway? I began to wonder whether it was out of pity.

"Where is your tree?" Majbritt demanded again. She had run up the stairs each afternoon, impatiently knocking on my door to show me which figurine she had found in her calendar. She only stayed for a few minutes but she was a whirlwind of exhausting energy, talking non-stop, desperate to share everything Christmas-related with me. I could see in her eyes she was exhausted too but that just spurred her on rather than slow her down. Annika had said, more than once, that she couldn't wait for the end of term; Majbritt was too wired and needed to sleep. I think it was Annika that was more desperate to sleep and two weeks without the school run had its appeal.

Majbritt's school is so new and clean. So open, light and airy. Nothing like the tired school we had gone to in Islington. It had been there since the mid-eighteen-hundreds until it was damaged during a bomb raid a year before the end of the war. The school moved to a different site the very next day. Nothing would stop school opening, not even a bomb. Not that we minded. We appreciated the normality in our very abnormal lives at that time.

Taking my seat along with Annika and Jan, I took the opportunity to have a proper look at the school hall. I quickly realised that it was only the foyer in fact that's a new-build; the rest of the school is quite old. It's obviously had a great deal of money spent on refurbishments and hi-tech equipment.

Annika and Jan were so busy saying *hello* to others along the row, in front and behind, and waving at parents a little further back, that they didn't notice a cheeky face peering through a gap in the curtains up on the stage. I did. She searched the room then, spying me, stuck her hand through and waved. A moment later, a different face appeared trying to locate parents. Then a third. A loud cough rang out and the curtain was hurriedly closed. The small band to the left of the stage struck up, the curtains flew open and a sea of faces beamed at us. Of course, Majbritt was centre stage and of course, Majbritt had the most tinsel in her hair and extra tinsel wrapped round her wrists. They sang their hearts out, then Majbritt and three others, all dressed as ballerinas, narrated the story. Their tutus, dotted with a thousand sequins, were of varying colours. Majbritt's was a stunning, peacock blue. The children re-enacted what I can only assume was a modern retelling of the Christmas story, with animals replacing the humans, and an angry farmer replacing King

Herod. Either that or I missed the point completely. It was wonderful whatever it was and we gave them a resounding ovation at the end. Then we were all invited through to the dining hall for mince pies and mulled wine; or warm Ribena for those who would prefer it. I mean, who would?

Eventually, the children came through, some more eagerly than others. We heard Majbritt before we saw her, leading a troupe of six girls in our direction. She shouted introductions, then they waved in each other's faces before dashing off to their own parents. As one girl left, she turned back to Majbritt saying, "Your Grandma is really pretty!" I nearly choked in surprise on my mulled wine – which incidentally, tasted remarkably like a warm, cheaper version of Ribena. Annika rubbed my arm, trying not to laugh.

"Well, they certainly didn't spend the ticket money on decent wine, did they!" she said under her breath. "Maybe next year I'll offer to do the drinks. Show them what mulled wine should *really* taste like."

I didn't doubt her. I'd had Swedish glögg at the Southbank Christmas Market some years ago. It nearly blew my head off. I think there was more vodka than wine, and my head was spinning for a good hour afterwards. Howard found it hilarious, of course, but then again, he was a seasoned whiskey drinker; it would take a lot for him to feel tipsy.

I got to taste Annika's Swedish version of mulled wine the following week when we gathered at hers to celebrate Sankta Lucia. Sabina and Filip arrived with Zofia and her husband, Matthew. It was lovely to see Filip again and endearing that he hadn't changed much in all these years; still as shy, still as eager to please. It's strange how some bonds never break; Sabina and I have been apart for most of our lives and yet we connect as if we saw each other just last week. And it felt the same with Filip.

I had dreaded that the conversation would turn to Rueben but it didn't. Nobody mentioned it; it was as if it had never happened. Which in a way felt so much worse. Oh my goodness, my head can't take much more; I can never decide how I feel about it. Something is missing, I know that much. It's not Howard. Yes, of course I miss him with all my heart but it's something else. Something much more primal.

Once Jan's work colleagues arrived and introductions were done, Annika lit candles on the coffee table and turned the lounge lights off, before disappearing into the hall. Instrumental music started playing from the cd player and Annika reappeared, holding the door open for Majbritt. Dressed in a long white gown, with a red sash around her waist, she walked in slowly, carrying a tray of biscuits. Balanced on her head was a green crown of artificial candles, flickering in the dark. Her voice, clear and perfectly pitched, sang songs I had heard her practice for the past week or more, in her native tongue. As she continued to sing, she offered each of us biscuits from the tray, walking slowly among us. Annika followed slowly behind with another tray; this one filled with small glass cups of warm glögg, with fat, wine soaked raisins and almonds swimming in each one. Just one sip told me Annika had chosen the best red wine, and she hadn't skimped on the additional vodka.

Once Majbritt had finished her renditions, she fetched another tray to offer round, insisting everybody *had* to try the 'lussekatter' buns she had baked especially for us. Watching her embrace her cultural traditions so enthusiastically, really touched my heart. I watched Sabina, delighting as much as I was in the whole spectacle. Maybe it reminded her too of our

Hanukkah celebrations. Yes, the songs are different as is the food and drink, but it's the whole feeling of unity, of joy, of celebration; that is the same. It's been a long time since I celebrated anything like that. A long, long time.

Before Sabina and her family took their leave, she summoned Annika and myself into a corner for a word, thanking Annika for such a wonderful evening.

"Do either of you have plans for New Year? Only we have decided – because of you, Bella – to have a big party to celebrate. And I have invited Leon and Janet, and Arno's wife, Fiona. Leon phoned back today to say they are all travelling down and so looking forward to it. We can put you all up, there's plenty of room. They'll stay for a few days, so you're welcome to do the same." She was addressing me more than Annika but was making a point of including her as if she were family too. And so it was agreed without much deliberation, that we would all stay for two nights with her. Sabina asked if Annika could bring some of the baked goods we'd just eaten; she had been so taken with the whole taste of Swedish Christmas.

Going out into the hall, I noticed Jan and Filip deep in discussion, both with the same serious expression. Filip spotted me and gave an awkward smile.

"Ah, Kristabel, has Sabina spoken to you about New Year's Eve? Wonderful! It's all sorted then." He hugged me goodbye, a little longer than expected, then shook Jan's hand, nodding. The other guests had already left as we congregated by the door to follow suit.

"Kristabel, can I have a word before you go upstairs?" Jan put his hand out to usher me back into the lounge. Majbritt was fast asleep on the sofa, her long gown bunched up by her knees. Jan followed me in, offering tea. Annika wasn't far behind, having waved Sabina's family off. A look passed between them that made my stomach churn.

"You've heard from him, haven't you?"

Jan nodded. "Yes, I have."

I swallowed nervously. "And?"

"And … he's coming."

"What? Here?" I stared from one to the other, my mind racing, my heart even more so. Annika smiled, Jan looked more serious.

"The fact is, I wrote to him. I got his address … well, that's irrelevant, sorry. I won't burden you with how but, I told him what you and I had discussed. It's taken a while for him to reply and in fact, the response was from his wife, Inge. They are coming over to meet you and so, I invited them to join us for Christmas Eve." He watched my reaction keenly. I couldn't move, couldn't speak. I could only imagine how scared I looked; I certainly felt it. What had I done?

"It's a big step for you all, so I hope you don't mind that I made the decision for you. I think it would be best for you to have support when it happens. Yes?"

I nodded. Annika put a cup of tea in my hands.

"Drink that. Biscuit? Bun?" They sat patiently waiting while I grappled with the news.

"So, Rueben and his wife are coming *here* for Christmas?"

"Yes."

"And did she say how he felt? I mean, did he … does he *want* to see me?"

Jan shrugged lightly. "I'm guessing the fact that he is coming is answer enough. It's his choice. Nobody is forcing him, are they? It's what he wants to do, yes."

I sat for a while longer. I'm not entirely sure what else I said, my mind was in such a whirl. Annika walked me up the stairs and came in to make me some more tea before leaving me in peace to think things through.

I wondered what he was thinking; how he had reacted to the letter. Was he pleased? Excited? Angry? Would I recognise him – would he recognise me? So many questions buzzing round in my brain and no end of staring at the street lights from my window could slow them down, or give any answers. Eleven days. How am I going to get through the next eleven days? I cast an eye around the lounge that lay in darkness; I hadn't even turned the light on. Majbritt was right; I needed a tree. I needed some decorations up, some festivity.

I hadn't really bothered with Christmas since Howard died; my heart just wasn't in it. We celebrated Christmas for each other, with each other. In the early days we would have family round; Howard's brother and wife, their children, sometimes his cousins. His sister and her family. We used to celebrate Christmas twice; a Dutch Christmas on December fifth and an English one on the twenty-fifth. But after Rueben left, the Dutch celebrations fell by the wayside a little. We acknowledged the day with a special meal but nothing more. The English Christmas became the tradition I adopted. The Dutch one just carried too many memories that made me sad. And Hanukkah celebrations were an even more distant memory.

Sabina phoned to say they got home safely and to confirm the plans for New Year's Eve.

"Are you alright? Did Jan speak to you?" she asked.

"Did you know?"

"Only on the way home. He told Filip before we left. I think Jan is worried about how you'll cope. I said to Filip that you're as tough as old boots!"

I wish I felt it. I feel like motherhood has been my nemesis. I never quite achieved it, any of it. Sabina wouldn't understand that. She and Filip had it sussed right from the onset. They're a match made in heaven. I struggled. I wasn't a very good home-maker. I wasn't a very good wife. I wasn't even a very good mother, not really. I was too worn out, too done with life, too disappointed. Not with Rueben. Not when he was little anyway. He was a dream child. Although looking back now I do wonder; why was he such a quiet child? Was he, in fact, just unhappy? Did it stem from such a young age; should I have seen the signs much sooner than I did? Did he turn to drink because he saw his father doing the same? Too many questions, with no way of getting any answers. I couldn't possibly ask any of them now. Too much time had passed and there's not enough time left to waste with my endless barrage of 'what ifs'.

Chapter Ten

As I predicted, the following days passed in a blur of apprehension and stress. In a show of support, I was bombarded with phone calls from Sabina and Annika's daily visits became longer. They meant well but it just added to my stress levels rather than reduce them. Marta sent endless emails, each one full of news, sharing her experiences during the Kindertransport anniversary on the second of December. There had been some big events (and smaller ones) going on and she had managed to attend most of them. She had met so many people, reconnected with some old friends and made new ones. She was full of reminisces; did I remember this and did I know that. I didn't think I could take in much more; I felt completely overwhelmed. I did, however, spend a lovely Saturday afternoon with Majbritt decorating the tree that was delivered the day after Lucia celebrations. I thought it would be harder – putting up decorations had always been something I did with Howard – but Majbritt made it easier. I focused on her and enjoyed her delight at discovering the treasures I had stored in my Christmas box. I was invited downstairs for more glögg and biscuits, and to light the fourth advent candle on the evening before Christmas Eve.

I had toyed with putting some of Rueben's baby photos into frames but that felt unnatural; fake, in a way. Too little, too late. I kept them out though, in a neat pile on one of the shelves of my unit. To show Inge. I was dreading it, I really was. I'd deliberated over Christmas gifts but again, it felt so alien. Gifts should be spontaneous; buying something that you know the recipient would love. Well, I don't know them at all. So I opted for some fancy chocolates and a bottle of Scotch whiskey. Then it occurred to me; what if Rueben still has a drink problem. What if he's completely teetotal and would find the gift offensive. So again, I wrapped them and left them on the side. I would just have to gauge the situation when the time came.

And finally, the time did come. I was up at the crack of dawn. It felt like I'd barely closed my eyes before I was wide awake again, long before my alarm was due to go off. Showered and dressed early, I opened the door as soon as Annika knocked. She looked surprised, then smiled.

"God Jul! Merry Christmas, Kristabel! You look lovely today." She nodded approval at my simple, wine-coloured, jersey dress, offset with a silver lurex neckerchief. Howard's cameo brooch nestled in the knot. I mustered a smile and reciprocated the festive wishes.

"Now," she said, getting straight to business, "they arrived yesterday evening and checked in to their hotel. Inge sent a text to say they plan to be *here*," she pointed to my floor, "at ten o'clock. I told them that we will eat at two. Usually, it's later but I thought that would give you four hours to talk alone before you come downstairs to us. By then, you may need rescuing." She laughed but I could see she was thinking practically. "Traditionally, we have presents in the evening but since we've had Majbritt, we tend to do that in the morning. You are most welcome to join us now, for breakfast and presents. If you'd like?"

I shook my head. "No, but thank you. I am far too distracted and I think Majbritt would want my attention and I just can't – not today."

"Absolutely," she nodded. She put her hands on my shoulders. "Good luck. If you need me, just text or phone. Or come down. Whatever. We're here." And with that, she hugged me and disappeared back downstairs. Too late, I spied the bags of gifts I had put by the door ready for her.

I paced until my knees ached, then I sat and stared out of the window. For the first time in forever, the minutes ticked by slowly, prolonging my agony. I saw the taxi approach and slow down. My gut twisted and my throat tightened. I couldn't look; instead, I went and hovered by the buzzer to let them into the building. I heard voices in the stairwell and realised Jan had in fact let them in. There were happy sounds of greeting, a little laughter – I guessed at Inge's – and then footsteps drawing closer. The door knocked. For an instant, I panicked and backed away. The knock was repeated. I took a deep breath, pressing sweaty palms against my legs, and opened the door.

We stared at each other in silence. It was as if somebody had freeze framed us, like *Bernard's Watch*, for just a moment but felt like a lifetime. He was completely grey – I wasn't expecting that. But those eyes; those ocean-blue, deeply troubled eyes, hadn't changed one bit. I could tell he was as shocked by how I had aged too. He gave a tentative smile, a sad smile, pulling his hands from his pockets in anticipation. I put my arms out and croaked his name. He held me tightly in his strong arms, my head pressed against his chest. I don't remember him towering above me; either he had grown or I had shrunk. A wave of emotion hit me, of feeling complete. I silently wept into his jacket, trying desperately not to make a sound. Not to release the sobs that clogged my throat. Eventually, he pulled back, wiping his cheeks with the back of his hand. He gestured to the woman standing next to him, laden with festive gift bags and an enormous bouquet of sweetly scented, red roses and pure white, Christmas lilies.

"Mama, this is my wife, Inge." He deftly relieved her of her packages so that she too could hug me.

"Hallo, Kristabel, how wonderful to meet you!" She spoke in flawless Dutch, her warm smile lighting up eyes that had been anxiously watching us reunite. I eventually found my voice and welcomed them into my home. I was shaking, almost uncontrollably, and desperate to sit down but they seemed content to stand for a while, surveying the lounge. Inge offered me the bouquet; I thanked her and they followed me into the kitchen. The silence was quickly stretching into an uncomfortable one. Inge finally broke it.

"This is a lovely apartment, Kristabel. Beautiful. And London is so beautiful, too." And we proceeded with small talk about London, their journey, their hotel. Inge had never been to London before and she enthused about the sights she was looking forward to seeing. She kept glancing at Rueben, flashing him reassuring smiles. I made tea and produced a box of biscuits that Annika had brought up earlier.

"A taste of Swedish baking," I offered. Prompted by my words, Inge disappeared into the hall and returned with a decorative biscuit tin.

"I brought some Christmas biscuits with me. For you." She smiled widely as she handed it to me. The embossed festive greeting in German that wrapped its way around the tin screamed out at me. I tried not to let my smile waver. I wasn't ready to raise the subject just yet. She was speaking to me in fluent Dutch and I couldn't let on that I knew of her origins. Not yet.

Inge offered to help put the tea tray together and carried it through to the lounge. Rueben followed quietly behind. His smile was slipping and a troubled look took its place. He stopped by the mahogany unit, studying the record collection

101

and the photographs. He picked up my wedding photo and stared at it for some time. It was a group photo, the traditional one that everybody has at their wedding. Inge joined him, making appreciative noises to me. Rueben quietly pointed out the reluctant, adolescent figure standing behind Howard's brother, barely visible by choice. Inge gave him a knowing smile and squeezed his hand.

"We were so sorry to hear about Howard, Kristabel," she stated. I shot a look at Rueben's closed expression. He carefully replaced the photo and was about to move away when a different photo caught his eye. He picked it up, studying the smiling faces of my family.

"Who's this?"

I swallowed nervously. "My family."

"A big family. Did I ever meet them?" He eyed me briefly, focusing on the photograph.

"No, no. They died before you were born."

"Ah, yes, I remember now. But surely ... all of them? This is you – here, with the other children. Who are they?" There was an edge to his voice – or was I just imagining it?

"I told you a long time ago; maybe you forgot. They died in the war."

"A bomb, right? That's what you told me."

I nodded, trying to pour tea with a shaking hand.

"But ... I'm sorry, I'm trying to understand. This is new to me," he smiled lightly. "A bomb killed them *all*?"

I nodded again, focusing on the teapot.

"But not you?"

I looked up suddenly at his tone. They were both staring at me, waiting for an answer. Inge looked awkward, sorry almost, and sat down next to me.

"Come and have some tea with your mother, Rueben. We have plenty of time for questions later."

He relented, replaced the photo and sat opposite us in one of the armchairs.

"So what do you do for a living, Rueben?" I had often wondered and had never been able to visualise him having any sort of career. He had never been particularly interested in anything when he was a teenager. I took the opportunity to look at him now. He looked well. Not ravaged by alcohol and drugs, as I had dreaded. He looked good. Well dressed. Handsome. Like his father.

"I'm a tailor."

I nearly choked. "A tailor? My father was a tailor!"

"Was he really?" Inge quickly replied, stopping Rueben from what he was about to say. "That's such a coincidence; my father is a tailor too. It's a family business, you know, the whole generation thing. My father, his father, his father before him. It goes way back. And my father took on Rueben as an apprentice, after we had met. So he's now in charge of the family business and I do the books. My father has retired – well, he says he's retired but he keeps 'helping out'. They never can retire, these businessmen!"

I found myself smiling a genuine smile listening to Inge. The way she speaks about her family is heart-warming, and so surprising. To me anyway.

"So where do you live?" I was aware that my voice went up an octave, trying to sound as casual as I could.

"Düsseldorf. My family have lived there for generations."

"You're German? But you speak perfect Dutch, Inge," I complimented.

"Ah, yes, I had the perfect teacher." She flashed a wide smile at Rueben. He gave a little embarrassed laugh and

103

smiled back. My heart flipped. That smile, that little laugh. I rarely saw it when he was young but when I did, it made my heart soar. It's abundantly clear that Inge is the driving force in their relationship. She looks after him, there's no doubt about that. And I think he relies on her. It's almost a role reversal of Howard and me. I suspect she helped him through some tough times. I bet she was there to support him battle his demons, his addictions. Suddenly, I was seeing Inge in a new light.

"And do you have children?"

"Yes, we have two; one of each. They are very keen to meet you. Both married now. In fact, we are soon to be grandparents! It seems strange; one of my friends is a great grandmother already and we're still waiting for our first grandchild. But we were late starters, I suppose. I was nearly thirty when I had Isaak. Rueben was thirty-nine."

I could feel the blood drain from my face.

"Did you say, *Isaak*?"

"Yes," Rueben interjected. "And our daughter is called Lena."

I gasped, startled eyes staring in disbelief at his defiant ones.

"You knew my parents' names?" I whispered. "How?"

"*How*? By following your trail, that's how!" His eyes flashed angrily.

"Rueben," Inge countered but he shook his head at her.

"No, I can't be doing the polite chat when there is so much to *really* talk about. I want some answers! I want to know about *you*," he pointed an accusing finger at me, "And I want *you* to know how I feel. So that's what we are going to do here. Today."

"Rueben, you're not being fair. This is a big day for you both – for me too. Take it easy, please." Inge turned to me, apologising.

"No, it's okay; he's right." I straightened up, finding the strength from goodness knows where, to face him squarely. I was still shaking inside. This was the last thing I wanted to do but at the same time, I knew it had to be done. Plus, I wanted to know more about why they chose to name their children as they did. Rueben was surprised by my response and for a second, looked uncomfortable.

"Were you ever going to tell me the truth? You didn't even tell my dad – your *husband* – that you're Jewish! Did Howard know?"

I nodded. His eyes narrowed.

"Right. But not my dad."

"No. You need to understand, it was different then."

"How?" he snapped.

"After the war, I went back to Amsterdam. I didn't know – I didn't think there would be an issue coming back home. But the Dutch didn't want us, you see. Not all of them but quite a big majority resented us coming back. And I can understand why. They had been starved by the Germans. They had died from hunger. And then we started to filter back into society – *our* society – and we weren't welcome. There wasn't enough food to go round. The city was destroyed. There wasn't enough housing for us all. And resentment was rife. So I quickly adapted. It's what I have always done; adapt, to be accepted. Fit in. I didn't *lie*; I just didn't give all the facts."

He stared at me, open mouthed, frustrated by what I was telling him.

"But to not tell *me*? It's my heritage! I am Jewish! I had no idea. My dad had no idea, none whatsoever. He said you'd been sent to the country during the war because you were an orphan. He believed that – your lie. But his mother didn't. She knew; she said she could tell. And your name – not a very Dutch one, she said. That's what got me thinking, you see. I wanted to know. I wanted to know where I come from."

"So what did you do?"

"I started looking for records. It wasn't easy. It took a long time. But I found your parents, where they were born, where they married. That's when I realised their religion." He looked at me, his expression softening. "They didn't get bombed, did they?" He sighed when I shook my head. He glanced at Inge, a fleeting look of helplessness crossing his face. She spoke for him.

"The thing is, Kristabel, we can't find any death records for either of them. We found some others called Ruebenstein; Isaak's brothers. But not your parents. What happened to them?"

The compassion in her voice was killing me. This was the most uncomfortable thing for me to do. I couldn't shake off the question playing on my mind. I was just going to have to face it. I took a deep breath and met her encouraging gaze.

"What did your grandfather do during the war, Inge?"

She masked her surprise at my bluntness remarkably well.

"He was in the navy. He was killed in nineteen-forty; his ship was torpedoed off Norway. My father doesn't remember him; he was only two at the time. He has two older siblings, and they remember him a little. If you're asking me if I am proud of what my country did during the war, then the answer is absolutely not. And I can honestly say, I don't know anybody who thinks otherwise. My great grandfather helped raise my father, and he saw terrible things during the war. Appalling things that he never got over, never came to terms with. He had no part of it." She regarded me for a moment. "Does that help?"

I felt terrible; I think she could see that. I apologised. She told me not to and then reiterated her earlier question. Rueben leaned forward, willing me with his eyes to tell them.

"My father died when ..." I hesitated, searching for an alternative word.

"You can say *Germans*; I really won't be offended, Kristabel."

"He died when the Germans first arrived in Amsterdam." They looked at each other.

"Are you sure? Was he transported? Because we found no records."

"I'm sure. I was there when they shot him. Bits flew out from his head and his blood was everywhere, so, yes, I'm sure." I noticed Rueben flinch but I didn't look at him. "And my mother died in Belsen, in nineteen forty-four. And yes, I'm sure. A woman who was with her came to find me. But you're right; there are no records. I didn't find out about her for many years – twenty, in fact."

Rueben stood up, running a hand through his hair. He beckoned for me to get up and he gave me such a bear hug, not wanting to let go.

"How could I tell you that, Rueben? You were a child," I whispered.

"I don't know," he whispered back, "But I wish you had."

We sat down again and this time he sat next to me. Inge stood up to make more tea. Rueben looked round the room, nodding, deep in thought. He turned to me.

"I was so angry with you. Howard was a rebound after my dad left and I couldn't believe you were stupid enough to marry him." He pulled a resigned face. "But I guess I was wrong about that."

"Yes, you were. But in fact, it was your father that was the rebound, and yes, I *was* stupid enough to marry *him.* I was in love you see, before I met your father." I watched him process what I was telling him, a look of agitation growing. "You were the only good thing that came out of that marriage. It broke my heart that you couldn't see that."

"You didn't tell me. How could I know? If you don't tell me, I can only guess; draw my own conclusions. You didn't tell me anything. Were you ever going to tell me?"

I didn't know how to answer that. '*Yes, if you'd stuck around*,' or, '*yes, if you hadn't been so stoned*.' I left it unanswered. He stared at me for a while, then dropped his gaze. "You should've told me what my dad was like."

"How could I? I tried but you wouldn't listen. You were so young and you idolised him. He was a good father. He was a good husband. Just not a very faithful one."

Rueben snorted. "You see! You're still lying. He was a *terrible* father, a *terrible* husband." He paused, contemplating his next words. "He threw me out, shortly after I got back to Amsterdam."

"Why?" I couldn't hide my surprise.

"I came home from school one afternoon and found him in bed with the neighbour. I was so disgusted. He was like an animal. And when he saw me in the room, he lunged at me and gave me a black eye. I don't think he even realised it was me – I think he thought it was her husband. Anyway, I told dad's wife. They argued and screamed at each other, smashing plates and being all dramatic. She left. He threw *me* out. Then the next day she went back to him. I thought, *well good luck to the pair of you!* They deserved each other. But she didn't want me back either."

I just stared at him, my heart aching for that confused child. "Why didn't you tell me?"

He shrugged.

"So, what happened to you? Where did you go?"

"Nowhere. I stayed with a friend for a bit. His Mum was very keen to help, to get me through the last months of school but then she caught us smoking and asked me to leave. So I slept rough. I didn't bother with school after that."

"Oh, Rueben. So what did you do – I mean, for a job?"

"I became a master thief. I was very good at it." He smiled at my shocked face. "You would've been proud – I never got caught!"

I could see through his façade, his making light of it. Beyond that smile there was a desperate sadness in his eyes. I could see resentment lurking there too and I knew it would surface very soon. I could feel him building up to it. It's amazing how quickly you remember how somebody ticks, how their mind works. He's my son, after all.

Inge returned from the kitchen and we chatted about their children, about Lena's recent wedding and the imminent arrival of their first grandchild. I showed Inge the photos of Rueben as a child and she enthusiastically remarked on the likeness between him and their children. Rueben was less keen to look; he just nodded when Inge pointed something out and pulled that half-smile he does so well. He glanced at the other photos on the unit. I was deeply regretting not having any of him in frames. I was regretting showing the photos altogether, if I'm honest. I thought it would be an ice-breaker but it clearly bothered him.

Jan knocked on the door to invite us down, a broad smile on his face. Annika and Majbritt were at the bottom of the stairs to greet us. Annika held the door open wide.

"Välkommen!" she and Majbritt greeted in unison and then Majbritt skipped ahead into the lounge.

"Look at my new easel and paint set, Grandma! Isn't it wonderful!"

I didn't need to see Rueben's face; I could hear the stunned surprise just in the way they both silently caught their breath. I glossed over it by complimenting Annika on the tree and the decorations. The tree was decked with white lights, red ribbons of tinsel and a garland of Swedish flags snaking between silver baubles. Candles were lit on the coffee table and in hurricane lamps on the window sill. A silver tray of shot glasses waited on the low table. Jan handed them round. I noticed Rueben held his hand up, politely declining. Jan quickly grabbed an empty glass and filled it with apple juice, to match Majbritt's.

"Skål! Welcome to our home. And a merry Christmas to you all!" He held his glass up, nodded to each of us in turn and downed his glass. We all followed suit. I wasn't quite prepared for the fiery liquid that burnt as it hit my throat, but more surprisingly, for the sudden flash of memory that caught me unawares. A vision of my parents, a room full of family just arrived for a celebration, and the ceremony of them standing in a ring to salute each other with tiny, stemmed glasses.

Annika guided us through to the dining area of the kitchen. The table had been extended and laid with care and attention to detail. It's one of the first things I had noted about Annika; her attention to detail. The red linen tablecloth offset the gleaming, white fine china and silver cutlery. On closer inspection, the china was decorated with a platinum, delicate lacework motif, which caught the candlelight beautifully. Cut crystal glasses complimented the four cut crystal candleholders uniformly placed across the length of the table. The centrepiece – a basket of red and white roses, silver sprayed pine cones and green pine branches – smelt divine above the heavier aroma of meat and pickled fish. Dishes of food covered the table. I spied rollmops, meatballs, potatoes, pickled beetroot, hardboiled eggs, and a few dishes I didn't recognise but guessed they were some sort of meat in jelly. And then the large joint of ham, studded with peppercorns. Annika had already forewarned me of it, hoping I wouldn't be offended. It was the one thing that had stuck from my childhood faith; I have never eaten pork.

"This all looks wonderful, Annika," I enthused. Inge and Rueben agreed. Inge pointed to the meatballs.

"I bet they're not from Ikea, Annika!" she laughed. "Isaak absolutely loves Ikea meatballs. Every time he comes home for dinner he says, *'can we have Ikea meatballs, Mama'*."

Annika laughed, shooting me a brief look. His name hadn't gone unnoticed.

"Thank you again, Inge, Rueben, for the beautiful flowers. That was very kind," Annika nodded to the centre piece. She indicated for us to all help ourselves, pointing out the various dishes. Jan stood to carve the ham.

"So, Rueben, what's your line of business?" he asked. Majbritt had been staring at Rueben, fascinated by him. She interrupted her father.

"You look so different from the photos!"

Rueben smiled politely. "Do I? You've seen them then?" I thought he looked pleased.

"Yes! I found them!" she stated earnestly.

111

"Found them?"

"Majbritt, eat up now," Annika said firmly. Majbritt chose to ignore her.

"Yes, in Grandma's box. You were her secret. She was very cross with me but then she said sorry."

Well, you could cut the tension with a knife. I think everybody held their breath. Except Majbritt, of course. She loves an audience. Rueben straightened up, focusing firmly on her.

"I was her secret? What does that mean?"

Majbritt laughed. "It means nobody knew about you, silly!"

"*Majbritt!*" her parents chorused. Rueben held his hands up.

"She's fine, it's okay. So nobody knew about me?" He turned steely eyes to me. "Nobody?"

"Not even her best friend, Sabina." Majbritt continued. Dear Lord, somebody stop that child.

"Who is Sabina, Majbritt?" he didn't take his eyes off me whilst addressing her.

Majbritt shrugged. "She's ancient, like Grandma. And she smells nice."

"Sabina and your mother were evacuees together, Rueben," Annika explained, passing the dish of eggs to Inge. "In Islington. Isn't that right?" she smiled at me. I could see she was trying to steer the conversation away but couldn't think how to. I just wanted the ground to swallow me up.

"In Islington? So, not the countryside of Nederland?"

"No," I replied flatly. He stared at me for a moment longer, then turned to Annika, smiling.

"This looks fantastic, thank you." He turned to Jan. "We run a small business in Düsseldorf. I'm a tailor by trade." He carried on the conversation as if nothing had happened. Jan followed suit.

"So you have a shop? Is that *in* the city?"

Inge joined in. "Well, it's a little more than that. Yes, we have two branches in the city but we're also textile merchants. It's been in the family for many years. So, Rueben oversees the tailoring side of it, I do the books and my brother takes care of the import/export side of it. Obviously, there's more than just the three of us. We employ fifty-seven staff altogether."

"Fifty-seven? That's a lot of staff. Business is good then!" Jan nodded.

"It is. And with the internet, the business has expanded so much. When my great grandfather was in charge, during the war, they nearly lost everything. It was very difficult for many years. So my father spent a great deal of time building the business up again. The client list. We had lost it all."

"Ah, I see. I suppose all businesses suffered during that time." Jan was about to change the subject but Inge continued.

"Yes, absolutely but ours more so. After Hitler came into power, it all went downhill. I think that's probably an understatement but you see what I mean."

We all nodded, murmuring comments of agreement.

"No, what Inge means is," Rueben interrupted, "her great grandfather was in partnership with his lifelong friend. His friend was Jewish. And Jewish businesses had to cease. And their reputation was such that everybody knew it was a Jewish business, so it was boycotted."

I was aware that all eyes were on me, even Majbritt's, although she couldn't possibly know what the significance was. I carried on eating – what was I supposed to say to that? As it turned out, Annika asked the question I was refusing to.

"What happened to his partner?"

Inge shot a look at Rueben. I saw it. I thought she looked angry with him for talking about it. She swallowed her mouthful and sighed.

"He … they … that is, he and his wife, two sons and their families, were transported to Lodz ghetto in Poland. And from there to Chelmno, which was …" she paused, aware of Majbritt.

"We know what it was," I said quietly. I felt sick. I couldn't believe it. My son is finally here and somehow he has managed to bring the horrors of my childhood with him. How is that possible?

"It broke my great grandfather. He could do nothing," Inge continued. "That was the brutality of Germany. They could do nothing. It was so meticulously orchestrated that by the time people knew what was going on, it was already too late."

"But the anti-Semitism was rife," I countered quietly.

"Yes, but not with everybody. Not everybody had those views, Kristabel. Certainly not my great grandfather." She looked immeasurably sad. Annika took a deep breath and changed the subject, while offering more food round.

"So, how did you two meet? In Amsterdam?"

"Ah, it's a long story," Inge started, not wanting to talk about it. But Rueben did.

"It's not *that* long. Basically, I was looking for my family. As I was saying earlier to Mama, I wanted to find my ancestors. I knew nothing about them. And so, I found myself in Düsseldorf and …"

"In Düsseldorf? Why? We're from Amsterdam," I interrupted. What was he saying?

114

"Well, it says Düsseldorf on your father's birth certificate. And the birth certificates of his brothers. And their wives. In fact, your mother was the only one that's Dutch. And you were born in Amsterdam, along with your younger cousins, Greta, Malka, Lea, Ernst and Jakob."

I felt like I had been winded, like I was about to be sick from the pressure. I stared at the sea of faces staring back at me.

"My father was not German!" I stated hotly. How could he be saying this? I tried frantically to reason with it in my head; tried desperately to search my memory for any hints that this could be true. I suddenly remembered the day he died. The way he had spoken to the German soldiers, in a language I didn't recognise. I remembered other times, when I would hear them all chatting together and I couldn't make out what they were saying. I just thought it was because I was a child; maybe I didn't understand grown-up words. It never occurred to me that it was a different language. Was that because it was the norm for me? To only understand half of what was said? I just accepted it without question.

Rueben was watching me intently. "How could you not know? They left Germany only two years before you were born. They spoke in German, they must have done."

"But … I can't remember that. Are you sure?" He nodded in reply. He was growing angry at my reluctance to believe him. I shook my head. " I just can't … I mean, I was only seven when I left. *Seven*. Can you remember being seven?"

He sat back in his seat, folding the napkin across his thigh, giving my question a great deal of thought. Too much so. He almost seemed pleased with it; I felt like I had walked into a trap.

"Let's see; when I was seven, you and my father argued continuously. It terrified me. Every day. On and on. All day, all night. Then one day you just walked out. Remember? I woke up one morning and you were gone. I asked my father where you were and he told me to shut up. He was drunk as usual. Oh, you came back – a week later." He paused, eyeing me with disdain. "A whole week! I had no idea where you were!"

"But …" I grappled for words.

"Oh yes, you said sorry to me. You hugged me, kissed me, then carried on as if nothing had happened. So, yes, I do remember being seven. It's when I learnt not to trust you."

I was mortified. He had spoken in perfect English throughout so there was no hiding from it. Now everybody knew what an absolute disaster of a mother I had been to him. I wish I could have defended myself; said it wasn't true. But it was. I did that – to him. I put myself and my misery first, above his wellbeing.

"I'm sorry," I whispered. "Your father couldn't cope."

"Yes, I got that."

"No, not just with life or with trying to be sober. He couldn't cope with death."

Sensing what I was about to say, Annika excused herself and asked Majbritt to help clear some things away ready for the next course.

"What are you talking about? Death?"

"You had a sister – or rather, you should have had a sister. She died, when I gave birth to her. And so, the weeks after her death were very difficult for us both."

His face dropped, his eyes widening in disbelief.

"What?" I could see he was trying to remember things, sort events out in his head. "Why didn't you tell me?"

"I didn't want to upset you."

"By not letting me understand. That's so much worse!" He put his napkin on the table and excusing himself, left the room to find the bathroom. I stood up too.

"I'm so sorry, Jan. Annika, I just need a moment alone. Please excuse me." And with that, I hurried out and back upstairs. I slumped onto the sofa, drained, completely and utterly. I couldn't believe that my father was German and yet, it seemed to make so much sense.

The front door opened and Rueben appeared in the lounge doorway. I closed my eyes.

"How can you not know anything about your own family? Do you write everybody off, is that it? As soon as I'm gone, you hide me away in a box. As soon as they died, you wiped your mind of them. Is that it? *'Oh well, never mind, best get on with life'*. Is that what you do? Is it?"

"Of course not! How can you say that?"

"Because I don't know you, that's how. I am appalled – disappointed – in how you have just forgotten about everything in your past."

"I have not *forgotten*!"

He paced the floor, then stopped by the unit and stared at the family photo.

"Do you even know what they went through? Your people. Your religion. They died for their religion and you have the audacity to turn your back on it. Why? How could you do that?

"They didn't die *for* their religion; they died *because* of it. My life was turned upside down *because* of it."

"So you just did as you were told and forgot about it?" He was taunting me, goading me.

"No! I told you – we adapted. When I arrived in London, I lived with a Christian family and we went to a church school.

Church of England. I didn't turn my back on religion; I adapted. I had to. I was a child, I was alone. I suppose, instinct told me to follow the lead because I needed to be looked after. I relied on Mrs Trigg to *want* to look after me. We all did."

He moved across the room and stood opposite me.

"You see, what I find hard to understand is, your family – your *entire* family – were wiped out and you accepted it!"

I didn't understand his point. "What else could I do?"

"Be outraged! Be so unbelievably outraged. Remember them. Do everything in your power to make sure they are never forgotten."

His words were like a slap in the face. Suddenly, I understood his point perfectly and I felt completely desolate. How had I become this?

"But you know *nothing* about them. Not even their nationality. Not even which language they spoke. For God's sake, Mama, why?"

I needed to debate that one before I could answer him.

"Howard – the man you hated …"

"I did not hate him!"

"He was there. At Belsen. He was with the 11th Armoured Division and they saw the worst of the war. They landed in Normandy, they were in Holland and Germany during the fiercest battles and then they arrived at Belsen. He liberated the camp that my mother died in. When he told me he was there, I begged him to describe it to me. *Begged* him. I needed to know every detail. But he refused. He absolutely refused to talk about it. He said nobody should ever have to know what he had witnessed. And however desperate I was to know, something in his face, in the way he said it, frightened me so much. I think he meant, if I *really knew* how and where she had died, it would ruin every memory I have of her. And he's right. My lasting memory of my father is a hideous one. Nobody deserves to die like that. And nobody deserves to see it. So I think that is why I stopped wanting to know."

We were both suddenly aware of Inge standing in the doorway. She smiled forlornly at me, then at Rueben.

"We're waiting for you downstairs. Annika's ready to serve the next course. Maybe we can continue this later? But up here, not down there in front of others. Rueben?"

He nodded and crossed the room, kissing her briefly on the cheek.

"I'll go on down then," he muttered, casting an unfathomable look in my direction. Inge watched him leave, then sat next to me on the sofa.

"Are you okay?"

I nodded. I didn't feel it though. "He's so angry with me."

"No, no; he's angry with himself, for allowing it to go on for so long. And when Jan contacted him and he discovered that Howard had died, it made him unbelievably sad that he didn't have the chance to make peace with him." She looked thoughtful. "Did you know Howard sent a card each year, at Christmas?"

"No! How could he? Did he know your address?"

"No, he sent them to Niels and he passed them on. And then after Niels died, his wife did the same. Howard wrote to Rueben when he first went back to Amsterdam, many times. Always considerate of how Rueben was feeling but also telling him how heartbroken you were. Rueben didn't get the letters or the cards at first, but Niels kept them. He did that much right, at least." She stood up, offering me a hand to do likewise. "I really don't know how either of you could have

119

left it like that. I do know that Rueben is very stubborn but even so."

"He gets that from his grandfather – my father."

"I think he gets that from you, too. No?"

I laughed lightly. "Yes, probably. Well; yes, definitely."

I followed her back down the stairs. Annika was by the fridge. She put an arm around my waist.

"I'm sorry, Annika, we are ruining your Christmas," I apologised.

"Nonsense! Absolutely not. This is fascinating. Like I said before, we should write it all down." She smiled, lightly kissing my cheek and ushering me back to the table.

I worried about how the conversation would flow after that but I should've known that Majbritt would dominate the proceedings. She told Rueben and Inge all about *The Lion King*, adding short renditions of the songs, and then all about her school Christmas play. They listened politely but I could see Rueben was as distracted as I was. In retrospect, we should have allowed more than just a few hours alone for our first meeting. I just hadn't expected him to have so much to say. To be honest, I wasn't sure what I had expected. I had certainly underestimated things, that much was clear.

Majbritt asked if she could show Inge her doll's house once the meal was over and they were excused from the table. Annika cleared away and brewed coffee and tea.

"So, Rueben, " Jan started, "maybe now you could tell us about Kristabel's family – your family. What did you find in Düsseldorf?" He looked to me, raising eyebrows to confirm I was okay with it all. I inclined my head. Rueben looked apprehensive, lightly rubbing the tablecloth with his index finger.

"Well, I went there armed with an address from Isaak's birth record and an occupation for his father, Abel. He was a tailor and textile merchant. I found the house. It was still standing, somebody was living there. I somehow thought it would all be destroyed but, no. I knocked on the door and they pointed me in the direction of another house, just across the road. So, I knocked there and Inge answered the door. Her father came to the door and as soon as I mentioned Abel Ruebenstein, he invited me in. They made such a fuss of me. His mother appeared from the kitchen – she lived with them for the whole of Inge's childhood – and she cried. I had no idea what was going on!"

I think at that point my stomach hit the floor. I had that fuzzy feeling in my head and my vision started to blur.

"Kristabel, are you okay?" Annika was by my side in an instant, reaching for my glass of water. "You've gone white as a sheet!"

Rueben silently waited for my dizzy spell to pass. I sipped the water, nibbled at the biscuit I was given and gratefully accepted the tea that was poured. I looked at Rueben. He gave me a half-hearted smile.

"You don't have to tell me, Rueben; I know where this is going. Inge's great grandfather's partner was my grandfather, wasn't he?"

He nodded. "Yes, he was. And Inge's grandfather who died in the war, had been your father's best friend. They grew up together. In fact, he was at their wedding in Amsterdam. I have your parents wedding photo back at the hotel. I'll show you tomorrow. It had been kept, not only because the families were so close but also because it was one of the last decent photos of Wilhelm – Inge's grandfather."

"I don't suppose they took as many photos then as we do now," Jan interjected, concern on his face as he watched me quickly dab my eyes. I wasn't audibly crying but inside my heart felt like it was breaking. More family gone. Family I didn't even know but should have. My own grandparents; that's such a strange feeling.

"Would you like me to tell you more about the family?" Rueben asked quietly. I nodded. He moved to sit next to me and took my hand in his. More tears at his simple yet deeply touching action.

"Your father's family had been in Düsseldorf for generations. Not always tailors or merchants. I think it was your great, great grandfather that started the business, on a much smaller scale. Then, after the nineteen thirty elections, when Hitler's Nazi Party became the second largest party in Germany, the family started to make plans to move. Your father and his three older brothers moved to Amsterdam the following year, to set up the business there. Isaak was the only one not married. Their sister, Ruth, and her new husband followed a year later. The two youngest brothers, Mendel and Aron, stayed in Düsseldorf to keep the business running there with their father. His sister, Esther, emigrated to America with her husband a few years before. The plan was to build the company there, and then merge with Amsterdam and Düsseldorf. Inge's great grandfather would carry on the business in Düsseldorf and your grandparents and youngest sons would join you in Amsterdam. But then Hitler happened."

"Why did they leave it so late to get out of Germany?" I voiced the question I'd asked myself so many times in the past about my family leaving Amsterdam.

"I don't know. I suppose, like everybody else, they couldn't possibly imagine what was coming. According to Inge's grandmother, there was talk of them all emigrating to America if things got bad. But … that didn't happen either." He studied my face for a long time. "I'm so sorry, Mama."

I shook my head. "Don't be sorry. I'm sorry you had to find out the way you did." I looked up. Jan and Annika had left the table and were loading the dishwasher together. I knew they had listened to everything that had been said, and I wasn't sure how I felt about that. It seemed like my entire life had been unravelled so abruptly and so publicly in just a matter of weeks.

"You were wrong about your father, by the way," Rueben said. "He wasn't a tailor. Well, he trained as one initially but he had a head for figures. He was the company's accountant."

We sat for a while longer, drinking tea and talking about the rebuilding of Europe after the war. After that, I sat in the lounge with Annika, watching Inge, Rueben and Jan build a complex marble run with Majbritt. I must have dozed off at some point and was woken by Rueben gently shaking my shoulder. Taking our leave and thanking Annika and Jan profusely for a wonderful day, Rueben offered his arm to help me upstairs.

"Would you like us to stay here tonight, Kristabel? We can sleep on the sofas." Inge eyed me with concern. She could see it had been an exceptionally emotional day. I shook my head, thanking her. I didn't think I would sleep well but I needed to be left alone to process it all. Rueben emerged from the kitchen with a mug.

"Try this," he encouraged, watching me with a pleased smile as I tasted it.

"How …?"

"Warm milk and whiskey, with just a dash of vanilla. And a spoon of sugar. Good?"

"Good," I nodded. "Just how Howard made it."

He nodded. "I remember. He used to make it for me too sometimes, when I couldn't sleep."

"He gave you whiskey when you were fifteen?" I couldn't quite picture it and yet it would be just the sort of thing he'd do.

"Mama, I don't think milk and whiskey was the worst thing I drank when I was that age! He was being kind. He *was* kind and I'm sorry I didn't see that. I didn't see how good he was for you." He pulled a face of regret. "Or maybe I didn't *want* to see it. I was too jealous, I think."

"It's in the past, Rueben. And Howard would be the first to say, *'don't look back; just focus on the future.'* And in this instance, you have to agree, he'd be right."

"Agreed," he said, giving me a hug goodnight. "See you in the morning, Mama."

I waved them off, hoping the night would pass quickly so we could start a new day together.

Chapter Eleven

I didn't think I would sleep but as soon as my head hit the pillow, I was out like a light. I woke early though, with butterflies in my stomach. Of a different kind from the day before. Now I was just excited for what the day would bring. We had definitely turned a corner and I think we had silently agreed to move forward, although I could see by the look in Rueben's eyes that there were so many questions he was still aching to ask. I would just have to let him and answer them as best I could.

I had decided to go all out and do the full traditional English Christmas lunch, with a little help from Marks and Spencer's food hall. The initial plan was for me to host Christmas day for Annika, Jan and Majbritt but plans were quickly changed when we realised Rueben and Inge were coming over. Annika had insisted we all celebrate Swedish Christmas together but was adamant that the three of us should spend time alone after that, without them. She was right, of course.

"And besides, Majbritt will be exhausted by then; too many sweet things, too many presents. Trust me, I know her!" she had joked.

The front door bell rang almost on the dot of half past ten, as we had arranged. I buzzed them in and opened my door to greet them. Inge climbed the stairs alone, smiling brightly.

"Rueben will be along shortly. He didn't sleep well; too much going on in his head, so I left him to rest for a little while longer." She followed me into kitchen and sat at the table while I made some tea. "How did you sleep?"

"Not bad, actually." I felt guilty admitting it. "Probably because I hardly slept the night before. Is Rueben alright?"

Inge inclined her head. "Well, I think he struggled with it all yesterday. When we got back to the hotel, he broke down. I haven't seen him cry like that for a long time."

I wasn't sure what to say to that. Should I tell her that he used to cry a lot when he was younger? Not out of sadness – at least, I didn't think it was sadness – but out of pure frustration at the world. At his world, at the world he was being forced to fit in to. He had always been a loner, an outsider; making friends had never been easy for him. And that became much worse after his father and I split up. He alienated himself from people, so that he didn't have to talk about it. I had hoped a new life in London would have been the change he needed but I couldn't have been more wrong.

I looked at Inge, checking her phone for messages. She has a kind, open face, with dark blond hair, kept short in a fashionable style. She certainly doesn't look fifty-five; more like forty-five, if that. There's a strength about her that appeals. I imagine she'd make an excellent teacher or counsellor. Aware that I was watching her, she smiled.

"Don't worry about Rueben; he'll be fine. He just needed a little alone time, that's all."

I sat down opposite her, sliding a mug of tea towards her and opening the tin of biscuits.

"Tell me about Rueben; what was he like when you met him?"

She gave a short, ironic laugh. "A mess. Very vulnerable. I think that's what attracted me to him. I was only young, quite impressionable, and he was ... I want to say *dangerous* but what I mean is, he had an air of mystery, of being untamed. Wild, I suppose. He was a big, big drinker. He smoked more cannabis than he ate food." She helped herself to the biscuits, chewing thoughtfully. "He told me he'd been addicted to stronger drugs; heroin, especially. He said he woke up one morning in a hospital in Amsterdam, not a clue how he got there or what was going on. The nurse told him he'd been found in a side street, presumed dead. Then she said, *'can I call family for you?'* He said, *'no, I have nobody'*, and she said, *'are you sure because' …"*

"Because what?"

Her expression changed and she looked at me with such a sadness. "She said, *'because you were crying out for your mama all night'*." Seeing my reaction, she reached for my hand across the table. I couldn't bear it. The thought of him all alone, and calling for me. And where was I?

"It shocked him, the whole overdosing business. He hadn't intended to; it's not like he was suicidal. Just careless, I suppose. But he admitted himself for help and got cleaned up. Or at least, off the heroin. But he still had his vices."

"And does he still?"

"Oh God, no! No, when I met him, I fell in love almost instantly but I knew he was trouble. So I said, *'if you want a serious relationship with me – a future – you need to be off the dope and off the alcohol. Otherwise, we won't have a future.'* And I was absolutely clear about that. Thank God, he loved me too! He did it. It took a while, it took a lot of hard work on his part. He stopped drinking, he gave up the drugs. He went to night school and worked for my father during the day. He threw himself into it completely." She smiled again, a warmth in her eyes when she talked about him. I like her.

"So you saved him, then."

"Well, yes, I suppose I did."

I squeezed her hand. "Thank you, Inge."

"What for?"

"For being there for him. For looking after him. For being the person I wasn't."

She shook her head. "Don't think like that. From what he told me, he wasn't the easiest child. And I've met his father, so I know what you had to contend with!"

"You met him? But I thought he threw Rueben out?"

"Yes, he did. But once Rueben was sober, he went back to visit him. I think more to show him what he had achieved – and to introduce me. But after that, we didn't see much of him at all. Once every few years Rueben would go back; sometimes he'd bring me along but not the children. And Niels never showed any interest, never asked about them or indicated that he wanted to meet them. Such a cold man. A sad, cold man. But Rueben hated going back there, to Amsterdam. We never stayed; he would do a round trip in the car. He could never settle until he was back in Düsseldorf. I think it's the only place he feels happy. Himself."

We sat in silence for a while, both thinking about what she'd said. I couldn't ever imagine feeling comfortable in Germany but then again, Rueben wouldn't have that deep-rooted fear of the country that I had. I'm slowly trying to come to terms with the fact that Germany is the country of my family's origins. And that is such a strange and challenging concept.

Rueben arrived an hour later, by which time Inge had shown me thousands of photos on her iPad. I was staring at images of their children – a fast-forward through time – as they grew from toddlers to adults and not once did I think, *that's my grandchildren*. I feel so detached from them. Which isn't surprising, surely? I've never met them, never known anything about them; I didn't even know their names until twenty-four hours ago. That's another thing I would have to get used to. I was starting to feel incredibly overwhelmed again.

"I had just assumed my family were Dutch but now that you've told me this, there are so many questions filling my head. The Netherlands was neutral during the first world war but obviously Germany wasn't, so did my grandfather serve in that war?"

Inge nodded. "Yes, he did."

"For Germany?"

They both nodded. Oh, the irony.

We were sitting round my table, full from Christmas lunch. Inge was so taken with the Christmas pudding and was eating a second helping. Rueben had been filling me in with a more detailed account of my family history and how he had traced it. The one thing that had eluded him was finding my great aunt Esther who had emigrated to America in the late nineteen-twenties. I don't remember ever being told about her. Or my father's two younger brothers.

"I found their marriage record at the local church but none of Inge's family knew where they moved to and when I typed in his name, Abraham Friedman, to do a search on American records, over fifty-eight *thousand* possible matches came up. I won't be beaten though; one day I'll find them. Who knows, we may have family in America!"

"Rueben, the photo," Inge prompted.

"Ah, yes!" He disappeared into the hall, returning with an A4 envelope. "I would have got it framed for you but I wasn't sure what you'd like."

"Perhaps we could go shopping together this week for one?" Inge added. The anticipation, watching Rueben

129

carefully tip the photograph out, was huge. I suddenly felt ridiculously nervous. I let out a choked gasp of surprise.

"I know this photo! I know this so well." I quickly wiped my hands with a napkin and carefully cradled my parents in my hands, drinking in the image of them. Their joyful smiles radiated and my senses were hit with a dozen memories. I could hear their voices so clearly, chatting brightly as they stood at the sink, washing up together. I could smell his heavy over coat; a mingle of tobacco and spicy aftershave. I could see her dark eyes; soft and reassuring as she sang me to sleep.

"You've seen their wedding photo before? I did wonder," Inge stood behind me, resting a hand on my shoulder. Rueben sat next to me, smiling at my reaction. I wanted to cry, to laugh, to kiss their faces. I didn't feel sad, strangely, I just felt relieved to have the photo back in my life. It had always taken pride of place on our living room mantlepiece.

"Obviously, these are my parents – your grandparents – and this is Sander. I always thought he was the oldest but I'm guessing that Abel was, as he had the same name as their father." I looked to Rueben for an answer. He nodded.

"Yes, Abel was a year older than Sander, then Markus, then Ruth, your father, Mendel and the youngest, Aron. Here – that's Mendel and that's Aron," he pointed, "And this is your grandfather, Abel, and grandmother, Selma."

I mouthed their names, staring at the faces I knew of old and yet never realised who they were.

"And who's this?"

"That's *my* grandfather, Wilhelm. And next to him, my grandmother."

I turned to look at Inge. "Your grandfather was Clark Gable?"

She laughed in confused surprise. I explained. "I was convinced when I was younger that he," I lightly tapped Wilhelm's face, "was Clark Gable. And I thought my father looked like Cary Grant. Those two were my Hollywood idols. Oh, I don't mean the *real* Clark Gable and Cary Grant, no; I mean these two. So handsome." We all stared at the photo for a while longer.

"Did you ever notice how much Howard looked like your father?" Rueben asked softly. I nodded.

"Yes, I did. Of course I did. He had my father's temperament too. So calm, so kind. So caring." I could feel my bottom lip and chin shake with the effort of holding back tears. Sobs aching to erupt from my strangled throat at the thought of Howard. This was the photo I had always wished I could show him. I had my family photo but this wedding photo by comparison, is much more of a likeness of my family – how I remember them. Laughing, carefree, with such a happiness emanating from their very beings. The family photo, when we had all gathered for Hanukkah at my mother's childhood home, was more sombre. The adults anyway. The cousins, not so much. We were blissfully unaware of what was coming but over the years and with the benefit of hindsight, I could see the strain, the foreboding, etched into the adults faces. That was our last Hanukkah before our country was invaded.

It had never occurred to me before why we always gathered at my maternal grandparents home for family occasions. My grandmother treated all of my cousins equally and I had just assumed she was everyone's grandmother. I don't know why I had never thought about it before; I was their only actual grandchild.

I stared at the photo of my father's parents. There was something so familiar about them. Abel's sons certainly took

131

after him, in looks and physique. And I could see Selma in Ruth.

"What happened to the rest of them? The families of my aunts? And Uncle Daniel? I assume they were all from Düsseldorf?"

Inge shook her head sadly and shrugged. "Nobody came back, Kristabel. Sorry."

I'm not sure why I had asked; I already knew the answer. I stood up, stacking plates together. Inge helped, thanking me again for the wonderful meal. She filled the kettle. Rueben picked up a CD case, studying the cover. He indicated to me, asking permission. I smiled and nodded. Gregory Porter's velvet voice crooned familiar words.

"Howard loved Gregory Porter. That was the last album he ever bought," I smiled. He gave a smile back of appreciation.

"I remember he always listened to Neil Diamond," he said. "All the time. I can't hear a Neil Diamond song without thinking of him."

"Yes, he loved him. Big fan." I was about to tell him how we had seen him in concert at the Albert Hall in nineteen seventy-two, and again in Birmingham in eighty-nine, but a look of immeasurable sadness clouded his face, so I swallowed my words. Instead I busied myself making tea, with Inge's help.

"When do you want to set off?"

"Set off?" I frowned at him, not sure what he meant.

"I thought – well, I just assumed – you'd want to visit the cemetery. As It's Christmas, I mean. And I'd like to, if that's alright with you?"

"Of course. Absolutely." We looked at each other, wanting to say more but not sure how to. He smiled that half smile and nodded.

"Let's have tea first, shall we," Inge suggested. "I think all this talk of families and the past has been quite draining for all of us. Especially for your mother, Rueben." She raised her eyebrows slightly at him; her way of saying to take it down a notch. She wasn't wrong. I was feeling like whichever way I turned, I was hitting the same dead end. The same finality. Except, I have Rueben here now. But he'll be gone soon and then I'll have to pick up the pieces all over again. Come to terms with more grief, again.

We sat back down at the table, steaming cups in front of us. Inge had helped herself to some more Christmas pudding and was slowly picking at it with her fingers, enjoying the rich stickiness. Rueben regarded me for a while. The hostility I'd seen in his eyes yesterday had gone. Now he just looked sad, tired. He watched me massage my aching elbow.

"And how about you, Mama; how did you end up in England? Alone."

I thought about it for a moment. It had often played on my mind; the fact that it had only been me sent over to England. Why? I was one of eleven cousins, so how was it decided that I would be saved? I was an only child – maybe that was it. Which posed another question that I would never get an answer to: was it by choice or did nature intervene, as it did with me? I read somewhere that placental abruption could be hereditary, something to do with susceptibility genes. I'm not entirely sure what it all means but I often wondered about it; wished I could talk to my mother about it. Every time over the years when a doctor has asked, *'does heart disease run in your family, any diabetes in the family, did either of your parents suffer with arthritis?'*, I am always stuck with the same answer: I have absolutely no idea. None. Not even their nationality, as it turns out.

"Well, it all happened so quickly. One minute, we were all leaving together and the next, it was just me. I was put in a car with a man called Peer. At first, I thought he was my uncle's friend, David, because I had been told we would be going with him. But Peer was a local greengrocer; he had transport and was able to get me out of Amsterdam to a rendez vous with David. From there, we came over by boat. David was lovely, very kind. He and my uncle Jusef were old friends from university. I had never realised that Jusef had gone to Cambridge University; that's where he met David. And then David took a job in Amsterdam because of Jusef. He was a civil servant. Then, when the German army obliterated Rotterdam, the royal family, the embassy and all the staff were bundled out of Amsterdam for England. Except David refused to leave without his girlfriend, Ola. She was Polish and had fled to Amsterdam the year before with her mother and sister. Her father had been shot in the town square; he was a teacher. They rounded up teachers, lawyers, civil servants – anybody with an education, it seems – and killed them. Non-Jews. Thousands of them. Anyway, David couldn't bring Ola with him unless they were married so that's what he did, within twenty-four hours. And they took me along as their daughter. There was a commotion about it but everybody was in such a hurry and turmoil that I managed to get through without paperwork. My 'parents' had their papers so I was accepted. Until we got to London. Then it was up to the same committees organising the Kindertransport to somehow find me a home and make sure I could stay. David paid for me. He was my sponsor."

"But why couldn't you stay with him and his wife?"

I sighed. "Paperwork. Technically, they were refugees too, even though he was British. His life was in Amsterdam; his home, his job. He had no address in England and so it was deemed impossible for him to be responsible for me."

"And what happened to him?"

"He and Ola stayed here throughout the war, in lodgings. Then they moved to America, to live with her mother and sister who had somehow survived and joined the mass emigration once it was all over. They wanted to take me with them but I was still convinced my mother would come back for me. So he helped out financially until I started work. We kept in touch, letters at Christmas, that kind of thing. In fact, I got my job with the Dutch Embassy here, on his recommendation."

"That sounds quite a daring escape," Inge interjected.

"I know. Of course, I was oblivious to it at the time but some years later, when I was older, Ola told me all about it. Things could have been so different."

"And you ended up in Islington?"

"Yes. When I arrived, the children of London had been evacuated and returned home once already and were in the throes of another evacuation. *We* didn't get evacuated again. Mrs Trigg opened her doors to families who had been bombed, and to me. She already had five children from the Kindertransport. We all pitched in, helping as best we could. I learnt to make beds from a very young age. She always insisted that even though there was a war on, standards had to be maintained."

I found out, after the war, that David had tried everything to get the rest of my family out but there was nobody left in Amsterdam that could help. He didn't give up though and eventually managed to get a reliable contact but by then they had already been deported. He was the one that broke the news to me about Jusef and later, Elise. He could never look me in the eye after that; he truly felt that he had let me, and them, down.

"How often do you come here?"

"Every week. I find it comforting. And I like to keep it tidy, with fresh flowers. Clear away the leaves from that cherry laurel over there. Then I just like to sit and have a chat."

Inge and I were taking a slow wander around the cemetery by Howard's grave. Rueben had requested a moment alone and was on his haunches by the headstone, disregarding the nearby bench. I tried not to watch but I was curious to know what he was thinking, saying. Was it out loud or all internalised?

""It must be difficult not having a focus, a place, to remember your family. Your parents. Do you wish you had somewhere to go?" Inge asked.

"No, that's different. That would just be painful, I think. Howard was ready to go. He was ninety-two, after all. We're ready to go at our age. Whereas my parents – it wasn't their time. It shouldn't have been. Their lives were snatched away. Howard died peacefully in his bed, next to me. His last moments were warm and safe. Comfortable. He drifted off peacefully. My mother was starved, frozen and petrified. Totally broken. I wouldn't want to be reminded of that. I mean, I can't shake that thought off but if I had somewhere to go as a focal point, it would just constantly reinforce that image."

"I'm sorry," she murmured. We had stopped strolling and were watching the back of Rueben's bent head.

"My great grandfather wanted to go to Chelmno, after the war. After they found out about Abel and Selma." Inge gave me an apologetic look; she clearly didn't want to let it go. She wanted to talk about it.

"Why?"

"To pay his respects. To see it – where it happened. He needed to go there, to help him … I don't know … understand, I suppose. To grieve. To believe it. I mean, it is unbelievable. That somebody could do that to other human beings. But there was nothing left of the camp; it's not like Auschwitz. And getting there was another issue, so he never went. But he wished he could." She smiled sympathetically at my heavy sigh, completely missing what I was sighing about. We had come to visit Howard; to my place of peace, my sanctuary. And yet she had managed, again, to bring up the horrors I strove to forget. Why is the younger generation so obsessed with reminding us about the war, as if we weren't there? Perhaps if *they'd* been there, they'd want to forget it too.

Chapter Twelve

"No, thank you," I held up a hand, shaking my head to Inge's offer of more tea. A wonderfully soft, mohair blanket rested across my knees, the delicate peach a good contrast to my chocolate coloured sofa. We'd had a rather awkward gift exchange on our return from the cemetery. Well, I had felt awkward at any rate but Inge seemed to breeze through it, delighting in showering me with gifts. The blanket, a pair of deeply padded, velvet, bootee slippers and a trinket box decorated with delicate, unfurling rose buds, put my chocolates and whiskey to shame but Inge had enthused about them loudly. Maybe a little too much so. Rueben, like me, had been embarrassed by the whole thing. I hadn't wanted to give the whiskey but she had caught me on the hop and I panicked at the sight of her extravagantly gift-wrapped parcels. I'd muttered something about wanting to give a taste of traditional whiskey and traditional confectionary, and she'd gushed that she would enjoy sharing them with their children. Maybe it's just me but it felt so uncomfortable and I just wanted it to be over and done with.

Having done her gift giving and tea offering duties, Inge excused herself, saying she had promised to drop in to Annika's with a gift for Majbritt.

"It's a traditional German doll," she confided. "I think she will love it!"

Once she had left, Rueben and I sighed simultaneously. He gave me a knowing look and laughed.

"I'm sorry, Rueben, about the whiskey."

"No, no, don't be. It was a lovely gesture. I'm sure Isaak will appreciate it."

We sat in silence for a long while, next to each other on the sofa. It wasn't a strained kind of silence; we were both deep in thought, reflecting on the events of the last twenty-four hours. Twenty-four hours – was that all it was? It felt like he'd been here for much longer.

"Why didn't you come for me, Mama?"

I stared at him, mortified by his directness. I couldn't think what to say. He didn't look angry; just deeply sad. His voice was heavy with regret.

"You have no idea what's it's like to be rejected by your parents, Mama. No idea. You completely and utterly destroyed me."

I couldn't speak. I couldn't find any words that would be of consolation to him.

"When Isaak was born, I had such a surge of protectiveness. I felt so paternal, and I couldn't understand *how* you could have just left me. Ignored me. I could *never* do that to my child!" His eyes flashed with a desperation. "I hated you for that."

"I know. I hated myself for it."

"Why did you do it?"

"I don't know. Maybe because it was a struggle trying to be a mother with no role model …"

"No! Don't give me that! I've met others that lost their parents and they did fine themselves. If anything, they overcompensated for it. They showered their children with love. Suffocating, almost."

"But you made it so difficult, Rueben. You were so awful to Howard. He did everything for us."

"Yes, I know. But … but at the time, I hated him too. I thought after my dad left, I could have you to myself. You'd notice me. I'd get your attention. For a brief moment, I had it.

139

And then Howard appeared. And you only had eyes for him, and forgot all about me again."

"Rueben, I …" I floundered. What could I say?

"I wanted to be the man, Mama. I wanted to look after you. I wanted to grow up and get a job and make life good. But I didn't get to do that. Any of it. And then, years later when I found out what happened to your family – *my* family – and how you were separated from them at such a young age, I wondered how you could do that; how you could let that happen to me. To us."

"I didn't think you wanted me in your life. Why didn't you come back when your father threw you out?"

He shrugged. "Stubborn. Too proud. Too annoyed that you'd been right." He shot me a sidelong look. "I waited for you. I thought, *she'll come back and fetch me home*. But you didn't. Whatever I did, I was just a child. The drinking and the drugs – it was an escape. A lashing out. But you're my mother; you should've known that."

Looking at him, at his childlike eyes in an adult face, filled me with panic. There's so much to live for suddenly, and I'm so acutely aware that my time is running out.

"I'm so sorry, Rueben. I don't know what else I can say."

"I'm sorry too, Mama. We've wasted a lifetime, haven't we?" He leant towards me and I put my arms around him. He's twice my size and yet he felt so small. He straightened up and took my hand in his.

"I think – if you don't mind me talking about it?"

"No, no, please," I smiled weakly.

"I think you were scared you could never be as perfect as your mother. And by being a mum, it made you a grown up and I don't think you were ready to grow up. You'd lost your childhood and I think you were still searching for it. That's why you went back to Amsterdam."

I thought about it for a moment. "You're probably right, Rueben. I was looking for my mother but maybe, deep down, I was looking for the past. For the time that I'd been robbed of. But, Howard – whatever you feel about him – he *saved* me. He saved us."

He nodded. "I know. Ironically, I *wanted* to be his son. I *wanted* to belong. But I was just too jealous of your happiness. And I resented him for making you so happy. I'm sorry for that, too."

We hugged again and went to make tea together. He sat at the kitchen table, fiddling with a napkin from earlier.

"That week, when you disappeared; I was terrified. I saw Dad hit you once. I thought he'd done it again; I thought he'd killed you. And I was too scared to ask again where you were. I thought he'd kill me next. He was so angry when he was drunk. So full of rage; absolute burning rage." He nodded thanks when I placed a cup of tea in front of him and took a seat opposite.

He'd been right – Niels *had* hit me. Rueben had been in bed, thankfully, and hadn't seen or heard us fighting. I left and booked into a hotel until my face healed a little. I hadn't wanted Rueben to see it but it didn't occur to me that he would worry more at my sudden disappearance. I didn't consider what he would be thinking or how he would cope.

"I found out years later about his dad. Did you know about him?" he asked.

I shook my head.

"He was a Nazi collaborator. One of many. Thousands, in fact."

"What happened to him?"

"He was executed. Shot."

"And your father?"

"Well, he was just a kid still and you know how cruel kids can be. He was tormented by the others. Beaten up, bullied; it was relentless. His mother too but she refused to cave though; she stood her ground. She said it wasn't *her* that was a collaborator and she would not be punished for his crimes."

I could imagine her saying exactly that. But I also suspected she wasn't as innocent as she claimed. He grimaced, reading my thoughts.

"She said something spiteful about you once. In fact, it was the last time I saw her before she died. By then, I'd found out about your religion and was asking Dad what he knew about your parents but he knew nothing. Then, she said you only married him because nobody else would take a Jew. He shouted back at her; he said he only married you because nobody else would touch him, because of *her,* and his treacherous father. It was the first time I'd ever heard him defend you. If you can call it defending, but you know what I mean. He never stood up to her. She was a nasty piece of work. I don't doubt for a minute where her loyalties lay during the war. She hated Jews."

"She certainly hated me. But I'm not so sure about nobody else touching your dad – he was a serial womaniser!"

Inge returned and we spent the rest of the day chatting and eating. Before he and Inge left, Rueben gave me such a bone-crushing hug, taking my breath away. I'm not used to hugs anymore. I get pats or head butts from Majbritt, and Annika occasionally gives me a light, brief hug. Howard's hugs were solid and safe; Rueben poured sixty-four years of pent up emotion into his. I could feel the relief in that hug – relief that we had overcome a huge hurdle and were on a path leading forward.

I sat by the window for a long time later, mulling over what had been said. My face and jaw ached from speaking another language so animatedly. I'd never really been aware of it before, or maybe I'd just forgotten. I had slipped back into my native tongue so effortlessly and yet, it felt alien after so many years of speaking English. And it brought back all kinds of memories; some good, some not so good.

The way Rueben and I have dealt with trauma in our lives has been so different. When I was faced with the prospect of being an orphan at the age of twelve, I just got on with it. Yes, I was traumatised; bereft, confused, lost – all of those emotions – but the over-riding feeling was to survive. To carry on. We all did it – carried on. We laughed together, we danced, we had jobs and worked towards bettering ourselves, our lives. Our grief inspired us to live. But now Rueben has thrown a shadow on that. Have I just been hiding all this time?

When his father left and he was faced with starting a new life in a different country with a new father, Rueben's reaction to the loss he felt was to blot it out; to go on a path of self-destruction. He was incapable of seeing anything positive about the situation. Instead, he allowed negative feelings to consume him and rule his life. And yet, he turned it around when Inge told him to. Could I have been that tower of strength that Inge has been? I doubt it, however much I wish to the contrary. The way I spoke to Majbritt when she found my box was very telling. I vented, not checking my tongue or considering how it would affect *her*, completely disregarding her age. I'm not sure I have ever really known how to talk to children, or comprehend what their young minds are capable of processing. It's as if I was never like that myself. I feel like I have always had to be an adult and yet there has been a child screaming to get out.

"She's wearing a very pretty dress and I love the frilly bit on her head."

"Her veil, you mean?"

"Yes but it's all bunched up on top. She's not wearing a crown like you did."

"A tiara," I corrected.

"Mmm," Majbritt nodded. We were sitting together on the sofa, studying the wedding photo. Propped up next to her were her new German doll, Simba and Pippi Longstocking. I could tell Majbritt was aching to touch the photo but knew she mustn't. Not until it's in a frame, I had already told her.

"She's very pretty," she concluded, looking at me. "You look like her, except she has dark hair."

"Ah well, I had dark hair too when I was younger."

"So, did she have white hair and a wrinkly face like you have, when she was older?"

I smiled at the simplicity of her question. "No. Sadly, she died when she was young. So she still had dark hair. It was a lovely dark brown colour, like chocolate. Very thick and shiny."

"My grandma had no hair when she died."

"No. I know." I patted her knee and stood up to replace the photo to its new spot on my unit. Majbritt followed me. She hesitated, a worried look clouding her face.

"Kristabel, we *are* still best friends, aren't we?"

"Of course we are! Why wouldn't we be? I thought we shook on it?" I held up my little finger to remind her. She smiled but it was an uncertain smile. The fact that she had called me by my name rather than *Grandma* was a clear indication that something was bothering her. I took her hand and sat back down. She fiddled with the fabric of my woollen skirt. I sat patiently, waiting.

"It's just … is Rueben going to be your best friend now?" she blurted. I caught my breath.

"Of course not! Rueben is my son, so it's a different kind of friendship. A bit like you and your mamma," I explained.

"No, it isn't, because he doesn't live with you and you're not really like a mamma."

I wasn't sure how to respond to that so I just glossed over it. We both jumped when the buzzer went.

"That'll be Rueben," I said, watching her face drop. "And Inge," I added. "She'll be happy to see you playing with your new doll." I masked my own apprehension. They were supposed to have been here yesterday, for Boxing Day, but Inge had phoned in the morning to cancel. They were exhausted, she said, and both had headaches. I could believe it; the whole experience was taking its toll on me too but something in her tone told me there was more to it.

As it happens, I didn't have time to dwell on it because Eileen called round, completely unannounced. She scolded me for not being in touch more often.

"We got your Christmas card, thank you, with your note of promising to arrange a catch up soon, so I thought, why not today? You haven't got anything else planned, have you?" It irked me a little that she should just assume that but I suppose since Howard's death, and before Annika and Jan moved in, that was about right. Nothing planned, nothing doing. Just waiting for the inevitable. So we sat and drank tea and ate the remains of Annika's Christmas baking. Eileen noted the biscuit tin from Inge; pointed at it and made an appreciative *ooh* noise, but didn't question it. Didn't ask where it was from or anything. Maybe she just assumed it was from Marks and Spencer's; it looks like something they would sell.

Eileen was too busy telling me all her news and not leaving much chance for me to reciprocate but that suited me. I told her briefly about spending Christmas with Annika and Jan, and an even briefer account of Majbritt's school play , before she interrupted with some other bit of gossip she was desperate to impart. I completely omitted telling her anything about Rueben. She didn't know him anyway; didn't know of his existence. A few years after he'd left for his father's and it was clear that he would not be back, we moved. Across the city. *'Closer for work,'* Howard had said. *Fresh start* is what he meant. New area, new neighbours. People who didn't know us, or Rueben. People who hadn't witnessed his self-destruction, or heard his fights with us, or peered through the net curtains to watch every time a police car pulled up outside our gate.

Eileen and Jack lived opposite us on our new street and we quickly became firm friends; even more so once their two children had stretched their wings and flown. Then grandchildren came along and Eileen and Jack moved to the suburbs to be closer to their daughter; downsizing at the same time, ready for retirement years. I was shocked, I have to say. Retirement was the last thing on my mind! But we moved too, shortly after them. Howard found this lovely apartment, minutes away from the city's hubbub and we thrived. Theatres, restaurants, art galleries, trendy bars with live music – it's all here. It's what we lived for. And so, when we did finally retire, we vowed to keep active, to enjoy every minute. I'm glad we did. It meant I had no time to dwell on other things.

Majbritt hovered by the lounge door, watching as I welcomed Rueben and Inge in. Inge greeted her brightly but the look of jealousy on Rueben's face was undeniable. I quietly told Majbritt she needed to go back down and as if on cue, Annika opened the door, about to call up for her. Majbritt skipped into the hall, stopping to push Simba in my face for me to kiss goodbye.

"Goodbye, Grandma! See you later! Goodbye, Inge, goodbye, Rueben!" she practically sang as she gingerly took the stairs, her arms full of toys. I watched until she was safely down, then turned to the pair of them with a bright smile.

"I'm sorry about that. She pops up most days when she's not at school."

"You don't need to explain," Inge dismissed as Rueben mumbled, "It's fine, don't worry." She looked earnest and wide-eyed; he barely held eye contact. He crossed to the window and stared at the street below. Inge looked concerned but smiled at me nevertheless.

"You must feel you missed out on being a grandmother," she suggested, shooting a look at Rueben's tense, straight back.

"Not really. Strangely enough, not until I got to know Majbritt."

She nodded lightly. "Oh." It was a disappointed '*oh*'. Rueben muttered softly, incoherent, then turned to Inge, forcing a smile.

"Are we going for that walk?" He extended the forced smile to me, guarded eyes not quite meeting mine.

"Where did you want to go?" I asked.

147

"We thought it would be lovely to see where you spent the war years, if that's okay? If you're up to it?" Inge suggested.

"Of course, yes. I'll phone for a taxi to get us to Islington."

Inge excused herself and disappeared to the bathroom. I smiled at Rueben. This was awkward. I thought we had turned a corner on Christmas day. Uncannily, he read my thoughts.

"I'm sorry, Mama. I have too many years of resentment built up to just let it all go in one day." He sighed. "This will take some time to come to terms with."

"That's okay, I completely understand. It's hard for me too." I wanted to reach out and stroke his arm or hug him – anything – but I could sense how closed off he was. I didn't want to add to it by reminding him that *he* was the one that ran away. *He* was the one who refused to let us help him. I didn't say it because deep down I knew that I should have done more at the time. I should have persisted. But I didn't.

Mrs Trigg's house is still standing, as it has for the past one hundred and fifty years, but now converted into apartments. It seems to be the way forward for so many of London's larger houses. The black and white, diamond patterned, tiled path to the front door has been left undisturbed and the gnarled, old lilac tree still graces the patch of front garden. That tree had always looked ancient and yet the brown, dried blooms indicated that it is still in good health and producing an abundance of flowers. In fact, I'd say it has fared better than me.

I pointed out the old post office, now a corner shop, where Leon used to work. Unpaid at first, just to help Mr Parrott out but then his assistant moved on and Leon stepped into her shoes. That's how he got the job in Scotland – through Mr

Parrott's cousin who ran a farm up there. Further along the street, we stopped outside a betting shop.

"This used to be the chemist," I explained, "and it's where I had a Saturday job. We all got jobs as soon as we could. I was going to secretarial classes, working here and also cooking breakfasts at the guest house. We all pitched in."

I had thought I wouldn't be able to walk far but somehow we covered quite a distance, buoyed along by my memories and Inge's interest in everything. I relayed the whole drama about the school being bombed, about the constant air raids, the air raid shelters and their unforgettable smell; a mix of stale air, unwashed clothes, sweaty feet and fear. The air sometimes tasted like somebody had left the gas on and other times, of damp plaster or brick dust.

"Our air raid warden was an old friend of Mrs Trigg's and she often came in for a cup of tea in the morning, relaying all kinds of news from her night shifts. She got caught in a raid herself one night and broke her leg when the ceiling fell on top of her. It could have been much worse, of course; she was very lucky. She found a kitten the week before, scratching around in one of the bomb sights, completely bedraggled and half starved, so she brought it round to us, hoping Mrs Trigg would agree to look after it. Which she did. We named him Charlie because he was black and white and reminded Mrs Trigg of Charlie Chaplin, and everything was fine until months later, 'he' had kittens! So of course, we had to rehouse them once they'd grown but it was easier than we thought. There were so many rats scurrying about that people were quite keen for a pet cat to get rid of them. Leon and Gabbi made posters advertising, *'rat catchers free to good homes'*. The post office took one and the pub took two straight away."

It was getting chilly. Inge rubbed her gloved hands together, trying to warm them.

"I thought it would have been terrifying living in London during the war but you make it all sound so exciting!"

"It was, in a way. I mean, we had no idea what was going on in Europe; none whatsoever. The adults protected us, which in retrospect wasn't that good because when the war ended, we were totally unprepared for the reality of what had happened to our families. To our countries. Actually, it was too much for us to bear. I remember Leon pacing up and down, like a caged animal, his rage growing, until he finally stormed out. When he eventually came back, it was obvious that he'd been crying. He locked himself in his room and wept for two days. After that, he seemed fine; the same cheeky, bright spark that he'd always been but we knew, deep down, he was hurting just as much as we were."

The following day found me back in Covent Garden, one of the *must visit* destinations on Inge's list. Thankfully, we didn't do as much walking but still managed to visit the Christmas market in Leicester Square and marvel at some of the iconic West End theatres. I quickly realised that Inge loves to shop and take her time browsing. Rueben seems happy enough to follow her lead and acted as if he'd never been to that part of London before. I did notice the look on his face when we walked past three homeless people huddled in a doorway. It was fleeting but I knew it had struck a chord.

We were in Waterstones. Inge wanted to find some books about London for Isaak and Lena. Why hadn't I thought of that? What a great gift that would have made, instead of the whiskey. The display table near the entrance immediately caught my attention. A selection of books, all following a theme to commemorate the imminent Holocaust Remembrance Day, screamed at me, *'we won't let you forget'*. Centre of the display was the book everybody was talking about at the moment, *The Tattooist of Auschwitz.* Anne Frank's *The Diary of a Young Girl*, was also there. I spied six books with the unmistakable outline of the Auschwitz tower in the background and three with children dressed in striped uniforms – or pyjamas, as that one book called them.

I watched a young girl pick up one of the books, reading the blurb on the back with such an earnest expression. She can't have been more than twelve, I'd say. How are children that young still interested in this part of history? I mean, I remember reading Anne Frank's diary when it was first published because it was so current, so relevant. I wished I hadn't – I had nightmares for months after. I think the epilogue affected me the most; it's certainly what stayed with me for a very long time. Of course back then, I had no idea that my mother died in that same hell.

I picked up a copy of the book the young girl had decided to buy. Another diary. Another young girl – Helga – a survivor of Auschwitz. She had a bow in her hair. Such a classic look of that era. It could easily have been me, or my cousin, Greta. She did look like Greta, in fact. Next to it, *Eva's Story.* Eva was from Amsterdam, a year older than Ezra. I stared at her face, willing myself to recognise her. But, no. She did remind me of somebody though. Curiosity got the better of me and I picked up a copy from the central pile and started to read the first pages of *The Tattooist of Auschwitz.* It wasn't until I snapped it shut again and walked away that I realised I'd been holding my breath throughout.

Exhausted from all the walking and full from our impromptu dinner in a wonderful Italian restaurant, I slumped on the sofa once Rueben and Inge had left, and pulled the peach mohair blanket across my lap.

"You won't believe what I did today, Howard. I think you'd be proud. Surprised; definitely. I *hope* you'd be proud. Don't worry; I think I'm brave enough now." I reached for the bag by my feet and pulled out one of the books I'd bought. Instantly transported back to a time I had spent a lifetime trying to forget, I couldn't put it down.

"Tell me again, Papa."

Papa sighed, smiling. "We leave early tomorrow morning and go to Uncle Sander's. Everybody will be meeting there."

"And then we go to England?"

He nodded, rubbing my shoulder and pulling my blanket higher. Mama was standing by the door, waiting to turn the light out. I could hear Elise and Jusef talking quietly in the kitchen; plates chinking together as they cleared away the supper things.

"Go to sleep now, Kristabel," Mama smiled, blowing me another kiss. Papa leant over and kissed my forehead then stood up and stretched his back. He looked tired.

"What about our things?" I suddenly thought.

"Already packed, already gone. All you have to remember is Häschen." He nodded at my bunny rabbit tucked under my chin. He was well-loved and quite possibly the oldest thing I owned.

"And my colouring book!"

"It's in your bag," Mama soothed. "Now, sleep!" She beckoned for Papa to leave the room and let me settle.

"So, are we all travelling together, Papa?"

He turned back to me, trying not to chuckle at my delaying tactics. "Now, Kristabel; I've told you twice. We travel separately but meet up in England. It will be exciting! A big adventure," he winked and blew me a kiss. I blew one back which he jumped up to catch in mid-air and patted it to his chest. He always did that.

"The monsters won't know where to find us, will they!" I grinned, pushing Häschen against my ear.

"That's the plan. Now, sleep!" They both waved and Mama pulled the door to, leaving it ajar a little way. I waited, watching her hand wrap itself round the doorframe to silently turn the light off. She waved her hand slowly as it disappeared again, and sang a refrain of a lullaby as she stole along the hall to the kitchen. She always did that. I turned to kiss Häschen before leaning my head on him. Heavy eyes closed and I was asleep within seconds.

My eyes flew open in the darkness. I'm not sure what woke me but a tight pain gripped at my chest. I slipped out of bed and padded across the hall to their bedroom. I pushed the door open. A figure was sitting in the chair next to their bed, watching them sleep. He turned as I crossed the floor, his features briefly illuminated in the moonlight from the window. Mama never closed her curtains fully.

"Howard! What are you doing here?"

"Go back to bed, Kristabel." His gentle voice made my heart ache.

"I can't. I have to tell them. I have to warn them about tomorrow." I shook Papa. He didn't stir.

"You can't, Kristabel. It has to be."

"Why? I can stop it!" Panic was engulfing me. I shook Papa again. Howard stood up and put his hands on my shoulders.

"You can't change history. Any of it. It has to happen this way."

"But Papa will die!"

"Yes. To save you."

"Save me? How?"

"Your life is precious, Kristabel. Don't waste any more time."

"But Howard – I don't understand!"

The room spun and everything disappeared into darkness. Somebody was shaking my shoulder. I opened my eyes. It was Mama.

"Wake up, sleepyhead! It's time to go."

I could see myself retracing the steps of my worst nightmare; unable to stop it, unable to warn them. Papa pressed himself against the wall, peering round the corner of our apartment block. A woman cried out for help. My heart sped up. Papa was about to gallantly and unwittingly walk to his death. But just before he did, he turned abruptly to Jusef.

*"**Run!**"*

My eyes flew open again and I sat bolt upright, gasping for air. I fumbled with the side light, the soft glow illuminating the corners of my room. *My* bedroom, now. I glanced at the empty space next to me where Howard used to sleep. Trembling, I went over the events of my nightmare again. It had felt so real, so current. I could *smell* Howard's aftershave. I could *feel* Papa's breath on my forehead. His voice had been so clear; Mama's too. How is it possible to remember their voices so precisely after all these years? After a life time. In all the times that that moment has replayed in my head, I had never registered what Papa's parting word to Jusef had been. I heard it but somehow failed to process it. *Run*. It was as if he knew. How could he?

Chapter Thirteen

"No, don't worry; I'll be fine. You two go and explore. I would only slow you down." It's true. I had woken up with every joint in my body aching. Two days of walking, in the cold, had not been appreciated by my worn out bones. And my nightmare had meant a very broken, fretful sleep.

"How about you rest in the warm then and we'll take you out to dinner tonight?" Rueben suggested, eyeing me with genuine concern. I nodded, smiling brightly.

"Or better still, how about we come back here and cook a meal for you?" Inge interjected astutely. She can read me very well.

"That would be lovely, thank you," I nodded. The last thing I wanted was to get dressed up and go out. Not today.

I cleared away the tea cups and debated crawling back into bed for a few hours. The phone rang. It was Eileen.

"I've spoken to Margie and she'd love for you to join us all for New Year's Eve, so shall we pick you up around seven? She's doing a late buffet, just some snacks really, nothing too fancy." Margie is their daughter; their eldest child. She moved out to Barnet shortly after her wedding, had three children followed by a very messy divorce. Nowadays, she lives more central with husband number two and the children have all left London completely – one as far as Northumberland. So, poor Eileen and Jack who sold up to be nearer to them, are stuck in Barnet and spend most of their time flitting between Margie and Jason, their son who lives in Richmond, on the other side of London. He never married but has had a string of disastrous relationships. Of course, I get to hear all about it whenever I see Eileen – which isn't that often any more. It's a shame because I used to enjoy their company but since

Howard's death, Eileen has developed pressure of speech. She's terrified of the silence that would ensue if she paused for breath. It's as if she's scared that I might mention Howard were I given a chance to talk. I don't think she's worried about me being upset – I honestly think *she* hasn't come to terms with it yet. After his funeral it was almost a case of, *'right, that's done; let's not mention him again'*. Very strange. Maybe she's scared that she'll be next; that Jack will die and leave her all alone in their Barnet bungalow with immaculate garden.

"I'm so sorry, Eileen; I'm already busy on New Year's Eve. I'm going to stay with an old friend."

"Really?" Her tone bothered me; I don't actually think she believed me. She chatted for a few minutes more before hanging up, not once asking anything about my 'old friend'. As if on cue, Sabina phoned to check that everything was still on track for our visit.

"I've spoken to Annika already about this, so I'm just letting you know too; it would be great if you all arrive tomorrow afternoon. That way, you'll be here for when Leon arrives later in the evening. And it will give us time to meet Rueben and Inge before the house gets too crowded. How's it going, by the way?"

"Fine, fine," I dismissed lightly, "but won't it be too much for you – all of us arriving the day before New Year's Eve? Won't it be too tiring for you?"

"Absolutely not! Besides, we can all chip in together, can't we? And please stay for as long as you can. It'll be like old times! Oh, and before I forget; can you bring that wonderful photo with you, of your family at Hanukkah. I told Leon about it and he'd love to see it." It seemed like an odd request – Leon had seen that photo before many years ago – but I

156

agreed, already making a mental list of what else I needed to pack. Just hearing Sabina's excited chatter, and the prospect of seeing Leon, gave me such a boost. Miraculously, the tiredness lifted and the ache subsided, which was just as well because Annika was at the door.

"I can't stop," she said, then proceeded to repeat what Sabina had just told me. "And then Jan, Majbritt and I will come back home on Monday evening. And either Zofia will bring you home when you're ready or I can drive down to collect you. It will be lovely for you." She studied my face for a moment. "You look tired, Kristabel. Maybe you should rest. Can I do anything to help?"

I did manage to doze for an hour on the sofa. It would have been longer but Rueben and Inge decided to cut short their sightseeing trip. Inge took charge, making herself busy in the kitchen, banishing us to the lounge with mugs of tea.

"Tell me about my family, Rueben. You said you've made a family tree online; can I see it?"

He looked startled. "Of course you can. Do you have a laptop?"

I shook my head. "I have a desk top."

"Even better!" he smiled. It was a genuine, warm smile. I watched him effortlessly work his way around the computer, logging in to a website.

"Have you ever watched *Who Do You Think You Are*? Well, this is how they do it." He clicked some buttons, then sat back looking pleased, gauging my reaction. It was a surreal moment, seeing my family's names in print on a timeline; some had a profile photo, which Rueben had cropped from the wedding one. As I studied the extent of it – not just immediate family but extended family too – I realised how

157

much time and effort he had poured into this. Unable to connect with his living family, he had made it his ambition to piece together his past one. My heart sank as I worked my way along the line. So many death dates within a two year period. So much stark finality. So much bleakness.

"Did nobody survive?"

Rueben shook his head. "No. Like I said, there are a few records we can't find but … you confirmed those deaths, so …"

"And do you think we *do* have family in America? I mean, is it likely? I don't remember ever being told of relatives in America. Surely they would have spoken about them?"

Rueben shrugged. "Forgive me, but you didn't even realise your family were German so unless they sat you down and told you, I doubt you would have noticed what they were talking about amongst themselves." He glanced at me, eyes widening. "Sorry, I didn't mean to sound rude; it's just…"

"No, no, you're absolutely right, of course. I think I missed an awful lot. And I also think I have blotted out things that I did know."

"Really? Like what?"

"Oh," I shook my head and laughed lightly, "nothing really. Just odd things, here and there, coming back to me."

He watched me for a while, expecting me to say more. What could I add to that? I feel I'm perched on the edge of a very, very dark, deep cavern; too scared to look down into its depths for fear of what I find. Maybe it's nothing. Maybe it's my mind playing tricks. Maybe it's the book I'm reading. Maybe I have left it far too long to question things. Best to leave it. *'Don't pick at old wounds'*, Howard would say. He was referring to the turbulence with Rueben but it was just as applicable now to where my mind keeps returning.

In return for Inge's delicious meal, Rueben and I insisted we clear up while she put her feet up in the lounge. It didn't take long for her to nod off; a satisfied smile playing on her lips. She had talked non-stop about everything they had seen during their stay, from landmark locations to little gems like the Dickensian-style antique shop they had stumbled upon, where she had snapped up some bargains. I studied the Royal Albert china cups and Wedgwood trinket box, not entirely convinced they were in fact 'bargains', but lovely souvenirs nevertheless.

"You must bring these with you to Sabina's. She would love to see what you bought. And just wait until you see her display cabinet! So much china – she's been collecting for many years, apparently."

Spent from talking, Rueben and I cleared away in silence. He stared out of the kitchen window, distractedly drying the dishes. He looked troubled.

"Are you okay?" I asked. He pulled a face; a half grimace, half apology.

"London doesn't bring back happy memories for me. I know it's your home and has been for most of your life but for me, it will always be my hell."

I nodded. "I can see that." I paused, following his gaze into the courtyard carpark at the back of the building. "But Inge's had a good time, so try and focus on that."

He nodded and smiled. "Yes, absolutely."

We fell silent again for a moment. "Thank you for coming, Rueben," I uttered. He stared at me in surprise, swallowing hard.

"How could I not?"

I sat listening to the silence long after they had left for their hotel. I'm not sure I like it. It's funny how quickly I have grown fond of Inge; everything about her. Her positive chatter, her forthrightness, her eagerness to show willing – all the time. And the way she adores my son. I felt jealous at first; I know it sounds ridiculous but there it is. Now though, I just feel content. Blessed. And dreading the day they leave again.

"Oh, Howard; why didn't you tell me to do the right thing?"

"Because you didn't want to hear it. *'Self-preservation'*, you said."

I turned to him, startled by the memory. I said that. I remember now.

"I did try," he added softly, sensing my turmoil. I sighed heavily.

"I wish you'd tried harder."

"You say that now but at the time, you didn't want to know. He broke your heart – every day. He pushed you away and in the end, he chose his father. Over you."

I remembered that ache in my chest; that panic as Rueben slipped out of my hold. Then the exhaustion that followed, combined with a sense of relief that the fight was over. His decision put an end to that battle. But the pain that followed was even harder to bear.

Howard watched me, concern etched in his handsome face.

"How could I try harder when you were already falling apart? *You* were my main concern and I know it devastated you when he left but it was *his* choice, Kristabel. You couldn't fight for him; not then. He took every ounce of your strength. You know he did. Don't compare how he is now to how he was then. Don't do that to yourself."

I reached for his hand but of course he wasn't there. Not visibly anyway and yet he is there, always. His chair is still next to mine by the window. We weren't really TV watchers; we preferred to watch life. This was our favourite spot at the end of the day; sitting by the window watching the world outside. A drink in one hand, his hand in the other, we would unwind to the sound of evening traffic. Sometimes talking, sometimes not. Just content in each other's company. I miss that.

"Has everybody got everything they need, now? Last chance!"

"Yes!" we all chorused. Jan had asked the same question three times and had rushed back in to fetch forgotten items twice already. I hadn't expected him to hire a larger car for the occasion but it was very much appreciated. I was offered the front passenger seat with extra foot room to stretch my legs and stop my knees from aching. Rueben and Inge were seated behind me, with Annika and a very excited Majbritt seated at the back. Majbritt had packed for a fortnight I think, judging by all her bags. She had never been for a sleep-over before; I know this because she had already told me six times.

It's a relatively short journey to Sabina's in Surrey and yet it felt like we were setting off on an epic excursion. Her village did not disappoint, with strings of lights and festive decorations along the main street adding to its rural charm. As we pulled into their drive, Majbritt banged on the window in delight at the twinkling fairy lights threaded through bare trees on the front lawn, with more surrounding the porch and dripping from the eaves under the heavy thatch. The cottage looked so pretty and inviting in the fading daylight.

A sea of faces were at the door to greet us and we were swept in on a tide of high spirits. Sabina had gone to town with decorations; garlands and tinsel hung in swags around the rooms and lounge fireplace. Baubles and bells suspended from the ceiling and a flamboyant garland of pine cones, baubles and red ribbon was wrapped around the bannister in the spacious hall. Noisy introductions done, I was quickly seated by the fire, with a cup of tea and plate of rich, fruit cake. Sabina sat down heavily next to me, nudging my shoulder and smiling.

"Rueben's very handsome, Bella, and Inge is so lovely. Have you had a good time together?"

I nodded. I watched the pair of them still standing in the hall, chatting to Filip. Jan finished unloading the bags and joined in their conversation. I blinked at the scene; so natural, so effortless. It's like we had all been doing this together for ever. Majbritt and Hanna ran into the lounge, hand in hand, closely followed by three other children. I looked to Sabina for a reminder of their names; Paul, Nik and Ola.

"So, you're going to be a great grandmother too!" she smiled, putting a hand out to steady Nik as he turned too quickly in his need to keep up with his older siblings. He hadn't quite mastered coordination and his bulky nappy hindered him somewhat. We watched him hurry back out of the room, with a determination that made us smile.

"Yes, I suppose I am." I know Sabina was expecting more of a reaction but I'm still not sure how I feel about it all. It's still very alien to me. Like I'm watching somebody else's family, not my own.

"It's bound to feel strange just now but give it time. You'll feel differently once you've got to know them all. Trust me."

"It's easy for you though; your family all live near you. You see them all the time; you know them so well. I will never get that with my grandchildren. I think maybe you're a natural and I'm not," I shrugged. Sabina shook her head.

162

"Not really. You learn as you go along. I struggled at first, after Zofia. I had terrible post-natal depression, although in those days, it was *'just baby blues'*, and you were expected to get on with it."

"What did you do? I mean, how did you cope?"

"I just did. I was so protective of her but horrible to everybody else. Nobody was allowed near me, or her. But it passed, eventually." I could tell by her smile that there was so much more to that story. "But that's why she's an only child. I didn't want to go through that again."

Rueben and Inge came to sit with us, putting an end to the conversation. Inge chatted easily with Sabina and within minutes they had crossed the room to peer into Sabina's well-lit china display case, admiring the various treasured pieces within. I saw Filip covertly summoning Sabina from the doorway. I could hear raised voices in the hall, excited greetings. Leon and Janet had arrived already. I put my plate and cup down ready to greet them, struggling to my feet; my left knee had seized after the car journey. Rueben jumped up to support me, offering both hands.

"Kristabel?" a gruff voice choked. I looked up, an expectant smile on my face. A familiar face stared back at me. Not Leon though. It felt like a fist slammed into my chest, winding me, as a vision of my forgotten grandfather – of my father, if he'd been allowed to grow old – crossed the room towards me. Everybody else crowded in the doorway, watching with bated breath. I stumbled backwards, blinking, trying to comprehend what was happening. Rueben gripped my arm to steady me. I saw the look of confusion, and of recognition, on his face too.

"But …" was all I could utter. Gnarled hands took hold of mine, squeezing them as he stared at me through watery eyes, his surprise mirroring mine. He shook his head in disbelief.

"Is it really you?"

I barely nodded, too stunned. Too confused. He snatched a breath, realising. "You do remember me, don't you?" he urged. "I'm your cousin. I'm Ezra."

I knew instantly, of course I did. The minute I saw him across the room, I knew who he was but couldn't dare to hope that this was real. I whispered his name on an inward breath, then struggled to breath back out. I just kept gulping in snatches of air as my chest and throat grew tighter, until the sobs could no longer be held in check. We fell into each other, weeping openly. Uncontrollably. Years of pent up grief finally released.

Eventually stepping back to look at each other, I laughed through my tears, embarrassed at the way he kept touching my face. He couldn't stop staring at me. I looked to Rueben for an explanation but he just shook his head, as surprised as I was.

"It was Filip and Jan," Annika said from across the room. "They got in touch with Marta and she found Ezra."

Ezra smiled, nodding. "It's true. I didn't believe it at first. Not after all these years."

"I don't understand, Ezra. I searched for you everywhere but there were no records of you. None."

He shrugged. "I didn't deliberately vanish. Well, at first I did, I suppose. But not for long. Where were you looking?"

"Anywhere! Obviously, I'd hoped to find some family back in Amsterdam but we looked all over Europe for you."

"Ah," he nodded, "Well, after the war I went to America and then to Israel, where I met my wonderful wife." He gestured to a woman standing in the doorway, linking arms with Sabina. She blew me kisses with both hands; I waved back. She crossed the room and wrapped her arms around me, kissing both cheeks. I looked from one to the other, trying to take it in.

"So, did you look for *me*? How come you didn't find me? Did you try London? Because I left shortly after the war."

"No, I didn't look."

I blinked, stunned. "At all?"

Ezra shook his head heavily. "They told me you were dead. *He* told me first, and then they confirmed it. I wish I had doubted them but at the time, I thought it was true." He touched my face again. "I thought I'd lost everybody. I thought I was the only one left." He started to weep again, quickly wiping his face and nose with a crumpled handkerchief.

"I don't understand. *Who* told you I was dead? You saw me leave for England! We said goodbye, and you said, *'see you in London when I get there'*."

"Oh, Kristabel; where to begin? Where to begin?" He slumped down onto the sofa, pulling me down next to him. He stared at me, then through me, to a time in the distant past. I could see the haunted look, recognised the infinite grief. I squeezed his hand, bringing him back. He smiled and touched my face again. "So many years. So many years, my dear Kristabel."

"There was a knocking at the door. Three slow knocks, followed by two rapid ones. Then a pause of five seconds, and another three knocks. *'It's them'*, Uncle Abel nodded and my father – Sander – opened the door." Ezra was sitting next to me, still clutching my hand. Rueben was on my other side. Filip, Sabina and Ezra's wife Chaya, were on the sofa opposite and everybody else was sat in a semi-circle in front of us, hanging on to Ezra's every word.

"There was Uncle Jusef, carrying Kristabel wrapped in a car rug. He stepped back and ushered my aunts in; Lena and Elise. Lena was as white as a sheet and Elise smelt of vomit; I remember that bit so clearly. My father looked beyond them into the stairwell but Jusef shook his head. *'He was shot'*, he whispered. *'Badly?'* my father asked. Jusef just nodded. My mother hurried the women into the kitchen and my aunt Maria took Kristabel upstairs. I wanted to stay and listen but was told to go and play with my siblings. That was always my job as the oldest, you see, to look after the younger ones. I heard Abel ask Jusef about the money, and then the panic when they realised it had all gone."

"I don't really remember this bit Ezra – any of it. It's like snatches of memory but almost as if I weren't actually there at the house," I said.

"Well, you were very traumatised, I remember. It scared me actually; you were completely silent. I was so used to you being the chatty one, the bossy one in the family, always telling me what to do." He squeezed my hand at the memory, smiling briefly. "And then your grandparents arrived. Everybody was there by then. I remember my father had gone into shock. He was barely holding it together. Remember how close our fathers were?"

I nodded. "Yes, inseparable. They all were but those two, more so."

"Yes. He was struggling. He had a wild look in his eye, a desperation, frantically trying to process what was happening. And I didn't help; I was asking questions. I was scared too. I knew something bad had happened but not what exactly. And I knew something worse was coming. I knew because of the fear in my father's face."

"The plan was for all of us to leave together, wasn't it?"

Ezra nodded. "Yes. They planned it all carefully but I don't think they really believed it was going to be necessary. As far as my father was concerned, the war wouldn't touch us in Amsterdam. He was more concerned about our families in Germany and how we could get them out of there, to us. And then Germany invaded Denmark and within weeks, they were in the Netherlands. So the plan was put into action. Isaak was the company accountant. He had, for several months, slowly been emptying the account at the bank. Even though the bank manager was a family friend – well, acquaintance – Isaak trusted no-one. There were rumours everywhere of spies flooding our country to help the German invasion. So he made it look like the company was losing money, gradually, which was hardly surprising at that time. And then the day before we were due to leave, he emptied the account completely. He had the money with him when he was shot dead."

All eyes turned to me as I took in this new information. "How do you remember all this, Ezra? I had no idea what was going on, not really. Only a feeling that something was about to happen but ..." I shook my head, searching my memory for any clues to verify his story.

"I didn't really know much either at the time; I heard bits of conversation between my father and our uncles and the rest I found out much later. We had an aunt in America; did you know? And she had been kept up to date with their plans. She had been the one insisting they leave. And then communication stopped."

Rueben and I gasped in unison. "You mean Esther Friedman?" Rueben blurted, eyes wide with anticipation.

"Yes! But if you knew of her, why didn't you contact her?"

"Rueben knew of her, not me. It's a long story," I smiled. I could tell by the searching look he was giving us that he was drawing conclusions not far off the mark. I wondered how much he had been told by Marta and Filip, or Jan. "Rueben never found an address though. How did you?"

"My father gave it to me. I was to get word to America, somehow, and tell Esther what was happening in Amsterdam – in Europe – and get her to send help. This was now two years after your father had been killed and we were still trying to find a way to get out. Looking back now, it seems a ridiculous notion but we were desperate. Round-ups had begun; more and more families were disappearing. People were shot in the street. It was terrible. Terrible."

"So, you survived the camps? Where were you sent? Auschwitz?" I tried to imagine what that must have been like for him. He shook his head.

"No, no, I didn't go to a camp. I escaped."

"How?" I watched him pause to blow his nose; watched how his face contorted with regret and defeat.

"Do you remember leaving, Kristabel?"

"Yes," I nodded. "It's something I can never forget. Saying goodbye."

He nodded, patting my hand. "You went with a man called…"

"Peer, yes," I interrupted.

"You remember him?"

"Of course I do – he saved my life! I remember I was crying for the whole journey and he kept reassuring me that everything would be fine. I believed him. I believed that

168

Mama would be following behind. But … did he not get back to Amsterdam?" The new thought struck me unexpectedly. "Is that why Mama didn't get out? Because Peer had been killed before he could save her?"

"No, no, that's not it. There was no more money to pay him. Your grandparents only had enough to get you out first. Then they all tried to raise more money for the rest of us."

I stared at him in horror. "You mean, they paid *Peer*? I thought it was David they paid, for the journey. I thought Peer was a friend, helping us."

Ezra sighed, watching my dismay. "I'm sorry, no, that's not what happened." He glanced across at Chaya. She gave an encouraging nod.

"What did happen, then?" I looked from one to the other. Ezra sighed again, taking his time to look at his audience before continuing. His eyes rested on Rueben and for a moment he seemed transfixed. His face softened. He'd seen something he recognised. I know because I've seen it too. It's a look Rueben has when he's intense, earnest, that is so like my father. Uncannily so.

"Ezra?" Chaya prompted. He apologised, took a sip from his coffee cup and continued, once again drawing everybody in to his story.

"Peer became quite a known figure in our part of the city. He had the transport and somehow, he managed to get passed the checkpoints in and out, without any trouble. He had connections in France who could get people over to England or hide them in the French countryside. It was risky but as he said, it was our only chance. *He* was our only chance. So families were paying him to get the children and the elderly out as quickly as possible. And finally we had saved nearly enough to get me out. The plan was for me to

169

get over to England – to Kristabel – and from there, get word to Esther in America. By then we couldn't send letters from Amsterdam anymore, or have any way of communicating with anybody. I was nearly thirteen by then. I was counting the days til they could send me. It was exciting in a way. Then the round-up happened. I was a street away, on my way home from visiting my friend. I could hear the shouting – angry German voices – and the chaos, and I instinctively ran towards it. As I rounded the corner, a hand grabbed me and pulled me off the street. It was Peer. *'What are you doing?'* he hissed. I said I was going home. He shook me. *'Don't you know what this is? What they're doing?'* People had stopped in the street to watch. Dutch people. Our neighbours. I didn't want to watch but I couldn't help myself. I saw them; my parents, my brothers, my sister, Kristabel's mother, Elise, Jusef. They walked out of the house, slowly, dignified. Not a word of struggle. I saw how my mother clutched Greta's hand. Jusef was last; he put a hand out to steady Elise – she was carrying little Ida – and the soldier shouted at him and hit the back of his head with his rifle butt. Jusef fell and as he landed, the soldier kicked him. I went to run forward but Peer held me back. Jusef got up and silently climbed into the truck after Elise. A soldier walked past the onlookers, scanning our faces. Peer was standing behind me and he draped his arm over my shoulder to cover the star on my jacket with his hand. *'Have you got the money?'* he whispered. I nodded and he held me close, making it look like I was *his* son. And then the truck moved slowly down the street, passing right by where I stood. My mother saw me first. She deliberately didn't look at me but she smiled for a brief second. A smile of relief. Then my father nodded his head and closed his eyes.

Neither one wanted to betray me by looking at me but they both wanted to let me know it was okay to run."

"And is that what you did? Run?" Filip asked. Sabina reached across and pressed a tissue into my hand. Ezra smiled awkwardly at the tears running down my face once again. The image of our family being herded into a truck – such a timeless image of Nazi-occupied Europe – was one I had never allowed myself to imagine. I couldn't bear the thought of my mother being ordered about or shouted at. There had never been raised voices in our home; she would have been terrified, especially without Papa there to protect her.

"Okay?" Ezra asked softly, wanting permission to carry on. I nodded, discreetly blowing my nose. He turned to Filip. "Yes, I ran. But not then. I was too stunned, too scared, and so I let Peer take control. As soon as the Germans had left our street, he hurried into our home and found the money where it had been hidden safely. It was a little short but he took it nevertheless and within minutes, I was lying in the back of his van, with a dirty blanket and old sacks over me. I had to hide there until he was ready to leave. I had no idea where we were going. It was a bumpy road and I felt so sick. I remember closing my eyes, willing myself to sleep but that didn't happen. The journey seemed to take forever; it was dark by the time we finally stopped. I heard Peer get out and give a low whistle. Then he opened the back of the van and pulled me out. I remember I stumbled because my legs were so stiff from the journey. He gave another whistle and flashed his torch twice. It was pitch black but I could smell that earthy smell from wet vegetation and I knew we were in a wood somewhere. Somebody whistled a reply. A flashlight was shone in our faces briefly and two figures appeared from the dark. It wasn't until they were in front of us that I realised

171

they were German soldiers. Peer had a tight grip of my arm, sensing I was ready to run. *Perhaps this is the check-point,* I thought, so I tried to calm down. Peer would show his papers and we would be on our way again. But it was the German soldier handing *him* papers – money. Peer leaned into his van and handed the soldier two bottles of wine. The other soldier grabbed hold of my arm and ordered me to walk. Then from out of nowhere, floodlights illuminated us, shots were fired and the soldiers fell to the ground. And *that's* when I ran."

"Was Peer shot too?" I asked.

"No, not then."

"But I don't understand. Was he selling wine to the soldiers? Was it like a black market deal he had?" I couldn't imagine Peer doing anything like that but I suppose in times of war, you would do things to get money. Ezra regarded me sadly.

"He was selling *us*. Jews. And, yes, wine or whatever he could get hold of."

"No! I don't believe that, Ezra. Surely you're mistaken. He saved my life!"

Ezra squeezed my hand firmly, shaking it. "Kristabel, you were seven – a child. You told yourself he saved your life. You believed it because you wanted to. He was a traitor. He was out to make money; that's all. And *he* told me you were dead. He said *he* shot you himself."

I pulled my hand away from his grip, rubbing it. He murmured an apology, suddenly realising he had been hurting me. His anger shocked me yet at the same time, made me feel inadequate.

"I don't understand, Ezra."

"I know." He forced a smile and drew in a deep breath.

172

"So what happened next?" Filip prompted. "After you ran? Where did you go?"

Ezra gave a short laugh. "About two hundred metres into the wood, before I tripped and fell. I knew I was being chased and he had a flashlight whereas I was running in the dark. This giant of a man effortlessly picked me up off the ground and held me at arm's length as I flayed about trying to punch and kick him. *'Calm down, calm down,'* he said, *'We're here to help you.'* I didn't believe him at first but there was nothing I could do, so I relented. As it turned out, he was telling the truth. I had been rescued by the Dutch Resistance. They took me back to a farmhouse somewhere – I never found out where – and fed me. There was a woman there, about Mama's age; she made up a bed for me and told me to sleep but I couldn't, so I crept back into the other room and watched them interrogate Peer. There were three men and the woman. I never found out her name but the men were Bastiaan, Sem and Dirk. Dirk was the giant. There were a couple of others in the house but not in the room with us. Anyway, they asked him questions – some of which I didn't understand – but it soon became clear to me what he'd been up to. He seemed quite proud of it. I think he knew he was going to die so why not die boasting! The Resistance had been watching the area for some time, after random bodies had been discovered – all shot; all Jewish – in the same patch of wood. They quickly realised they weren't in fact random but they also doubted it was the work of the Germans; it seemed too sporadic. Bastiaan had been tipped off by somebody about Peer; somebody who knew him and knew of his activities. So they had been following him for a little while and seen him sell spirits and wine to the soldiers. They always met at the same place, in the woods, not far from a farm

173

where the soldiers were billeted. Bastiaan had been told Peer was also being paid to hand over Jews, not just alcohol, but there was no evidence of it. So they lay low, just watching. Then that night, Peer had me with him and they knew they had to act, otherwise I would end up either on a transport to one of the camps, or in the woods with a bullet in my head."

I know I shouldn't have gasped but I couldn't help it. It seemed so unlikely and yet, I was starting to see how it could all be so true. I was a child; I was deluded. About so many things. Ezra gave me that sad smile again.

"I'm sorry, Kristabel, but this is what happened. He was an opportunist and a traitor. He always seemed to know when round-ups were happening; he would be there *'to help'* but in reality, he would sneak into their homes as soon as they'd been taken and steal whatever he could sell. Not that many had anything left to sell but he managed to find spirits and wine from somewhere. Anyway, I'd told Dirk about you and how Peer had taken you to a rendezvous, so he asked him about it. Peer just laughed. *'Ah, yes, she was the first one. That's when I realised how much those Jews were willing to pay. It's surprising how much money you can find when you're desperate!'* I jumped up from the corner where I'd been hiding. *'What did you do with her?'* I shouted. He sneered at me. *'I shot her. What else would I do with a filthy Jew?'* Then he turned to Dirk and said, *'I used to shoot them myself at first. Take the money and tell the families I'd saved them. But then I realised if I handed them to the Germans, I'd get paid double. And it saved me the bother of loading my gun. Bullets, you understand, are very scarce.'* That's the point when Dirk punched him in the face. The woman took me out of the room and this time I stayed where I was told to. I was shaking, I was weeping, I was beside myself. You see, I had in

174

that short time – a matter of hours – come to realise that I wouldn't see my parents or siblings again for some time and my only hope had been to be reunited with you, in England. And then that was taken from me too."

"Didn't you check if he was telling the truth? I would have checked!" I stared at him, trying to fathom what he'd gone through in those few hours.

"Of course I checked! But when I gave your description, they confirmed you were one of the first bodies that had been found. He'd been doing this for two years! Two years, without anybody knowing or stopping him. It all seemed to fit. They even described your blue coat. Your hair. Everything."

"*Blue* coat? But I wasn't wearing my blue coat!"

"Yes, you were. You always wore it. When you arrived, I saw you in it. You were wrapped in a blanket but I saw your blue coat. I know I did."

"Yes, yes, but I had to change all of my clothes. I'd been so scared that I had an accident. My clothes were ruined, including my coat. Aunt Maria cleaned me up and dressed me in fresh clothes from my case but I didn't have another coat so your mother gave me Greta's red coat. It was too small but at the time, I didn't even notice." We just stared at each other, clutching hands. Too many years had passed. He almost seemed angry with me, although I realise it was frustration at the situation. At a lifetime spent apart because of mis-information.

"Every girl my age had that blue coat," I said quietly. "Or had my hairstyle, my shoes. I am so sorry, Ezra. Sorry for your years of grief and sorry for the little girl who died alone. Nobody claimed her. I suppose there was nobody left." We fell into silence. I looked across the room, smiling weakly at

175

the anxious faces staring back at me. Annika had left the room earlier with the children; I could hear happy sounds from the kitchen where they were obviously being given treats.

"So, what happened to Peer? And what happened to you?" Rueben finally broke the stunned silence.

"They shot him. I wanted to do it myself but …"

"You didn't watch, did you?" I interrupted. He shook his head.

"No, they shot him while I was asleep and we left before dawn the next day. Then I spent the rest of the war with them, hopping from one safe house to another."

"You were with the Dutch Resistance?" Jan asked. "What did you do?"

Ezra sighed, glancing at Chaya.

"Well, at first I was in hiding with a few other children. Sem and Dirk's role was mainly to help save children; Jewish children. Bastiaan worked with them too but he also had other things he was working on. Obviously, I was grateful to be there and be looked after but I just felt so restless, so fired up with rage. I found it hard to just carry on being a child. We had to stay out of sight, not make a sound, just keep each other company for as long as it took to get rid of the Germans. Til the war was over. And obviously nobody knew when that would be. Every time I saw Bastiaan I asked if there were any jobs for me – anything to break the boredom. Anything to feel I was doing my bit. He shook his head for the umpteenth time and ruffled my hair, which was so annoying. I hated it! Just that simple action made me feel like a toddler! I swore at him, in German. The look on his face was priceless. *'Where did you learn to swear like that?'* he demanded. I shrugged. I knew I'd overstepped the mark but I didn't care.

176

This was the most excitement I'd had in months! *'How do you know German?'* he persisted. I just shrugged again and smiled." Ezra laughed at the memory. "I was a cocky little … monkey … and I knew it! *'I AM German,'* I said. And everything changed after that. They desperately needed a translator. I was agile, I could easily be smuggled from one place to another. I even ran down the back streets to another house once in broad daylight, completely undetected. Suddenly, I was in demand and suddenly, I was treated like an adult, not a stupid little boy with curly hair to ruffle."

"So you just did translating; you didn't actually fight or anything?" Rueben asked. Ezra inclined his head.

"I did what I had to do to survive. We all did. We wanted to get rid of them before they got rid of us. But," he waved his hands dismissively, "it's a long time ago now." The questions were getting uncomfortable for him, I could tell.

"I didn't know you spoke German as a child," I said, changing the subject. Ezra frowned.

"How come? My parents were German; yours too. At least, your father was. We always spoke in German at home. I don't really remember Düsseldorf, only very vague memories that have been prompted by photos."

"What photos do you have?" Rueben interjected.

"Only a few that had been sent to Esther. My parents wedding photo and a couple of me as a baby with our grandparents, in Düsseldorf. She had more of her generation and the generation before, and a few of our fathers when they were young boys. But none of my siblings, because by then we had moved to Amsterdam and posting photos to America was not foremost on their minds."

Sabina leant across to tap my knee. "Did you bring your Hanukkah photo?" she prompted. Exclaiming, I went and got it from my suitcase.

"I think you might like to see this," I smiled, offering it to Ezra. His face crumpled and he let out a whimper. He reached out for Chaya; she and I hurriedly swapped seats. I watched him study the photo intently, touching it – exactly as I had responded to the wedding photo Rueben brought – and smiling a sad yet content smile.

"Exactly how I remember them," he nodded after a while. "And now I can share them with you," he said to Chaya.

"Tell me their names," she prompted. "Is this you?"

"Yes! And next to me is Max," Ezra choked on his words and stifled a sob but it refused to disappear. Chaya watched him with concern, stroking his hand. I took the photo and held it so everybody could get a look.

"So, here is Ezra and these are his brothers Max and Jakob. Their sister Greta. This is me. This is Anna and Rosa. Their parents were Abel and Maria. This is Markus and Eva, and their children Edith and Ernst. And the babies were Malka and Lea; they were our aunt Ruth and uncle Daniel's children. Ruth was everybody's favourite aunt, wasn't she, Ezra?"

He nodded, wiping his nose again. "Yes. I think because she was the last one bar Elise to have children so she had always been a fun aunt; the one who wasn't too busy to play or take us to the park."

"Who was the oldest of the cousins?" Inge asked.

"Anna, then Rosa," Ezra and I chimed.

"So why was it down to you to get to America, Ezra?"

"Well, I was the oldest boy. The choice was that simple. It wouldn't have been safe for the girls to travel alone. Can you imagine?"

178

I shook my head. "No, they were both very gentle, very sensitive. Maybe Edith? She was more of a tomboy." I stopped short. Was I really doing this? Debating which one of them could have survived, given the chance. Suddenly aware of how crass I sounded, I turned to Sabina, lowering my voice.

"I thought Leon would be here by now."

She smiled. "Ah, sorry; that was a ploy to get you here a day early, for Ezra and Chaya. Leon arrives tomorrow."

Chaya excused herself and went into the hall, returning with an envelope. "Kristabel, take a look at these."

Sander and Hannah's wedding photo was not dissimilar to my parents one. The same siblings, same parents, just a few years younger. I smiled at Papa's radiant face, standing alongside the groom. Passing the photo on to Rueben, I stared at the next two. Ezra as a chubby toddler, perched on our grandmother's knee, with our grandfather standing behind. And another of Ezra at the same age, in a garden filled with yellow rudbeckias; again with our grandmother, watching him proudly. Judging by his stance, he was taking tentative first steps. I studied their faces, flicking between the two photos.

"I wish I could remember something – anything – about them. Did I ever meet them?"

"Probably not. I barely remember them. Just a distant memory and even then, that was after I'd seen these photos at Esther's."

"Hang on a minute," Rueben interrupted, scrutinising the wedding photo he was holding. "Inge, isn't this your grandfather?" Everybody turned in surprise. Inge took it from him, her frown quickly turning to a broad grin.

"Yes! And look; my great grandparents are here too, behind your great grandparents." She bit her lip and smiled at him. Ezra eyed me, frowning.

"What? What is going on here, Kristabel?" he said in a hushed voice.

"It's a long story. Long and complicated."

"Well, it's a good job we have plenty of time then, isn't it? I've talked enough; it's your turn."

I didn't want to tell him; I didn't want to explain myself, make excuses – because that's what my story felt like now. Excuses. And my mind was crowded with visions of Ezra dodging Nazis down backstreets; of my mother and aunts being herded into trucks. Of my cousins too scared to even cry. My story was weak and pathetic by comparison.

"The fire's lit in the other room if you two want some peace and quiet to talk while I organise supper," Sabina said gently. She squeezed my arm, giving me an encouraging smile. There was no escape. Why does everybody want me to bare my soul to them? I keep it all locked away for a reason – don't they understand that? Ezra's expectant face tells me *no*. And so, he and I made ourselves comfortable in the other room; a smaller version of the lounge we had all gathered in. Before I left the room, I saw Chaya sit next to Rueben and take his hand in hers, a maternal smile on her face as she listened to him. I had no doubt he would bombard her with questions about the family, wanting to glean as much information as he could from her.

I didn't think I'd want to talk but once I'd started, I couldn't stop. I told him all about London during the war, about returning to Amsterdam, about losing Lena, about Howard. And about Rueben. And as I spoke and he listened, the years seemed to melt away and I could see the Ezra of my childhood. He had always been my favourite cousin, and I his. We were like two peas in a pod; a little bit cheeky, lively, always up to mischief. And all the while basking in the unconditional love of our family. Then Papa was murdered and everything changed. I changed.

"And so, here we are. A right royal mess, as Howard would say."

"But I don't detect any animosity from Rueben. Sadness yes, I can see that in his eyes but nothing more."

"He's been very angry."

"I'm sure, and you can hardly blame him." He gave me a searching look, mulling over what had just been said. He chose his next words carefully. "I can see how it happened and I can see it from both sides. He was a child … but you know that," he held his hand up seeing my dismay. "All you can do is move forward. Embrace the 'now'." He squeezed my hand. "I can't believe this is happening; can you?"

I shook my head and laughed. "No! I'm just sorry that we missed so many years. Imagine if you *had* made it over to London two years after me. How different our lives would have been."

We slipped into silent contemplation.

"I still don't understand why it was me that was sent to England first. Why didn't one of the others go? Or you?"

"Well, the minute you arrived at our house, they thought there would be an army of soldiers following, banging on the door, coming for us all – no, coming for your mother and *you*. Jusef was convinced of it."

"Why?"

"He'd just seen your father shot. He was in a state of panic; there was this air of absolute dread. We all felt it. But they didn't come. Your grandparents did and they were thinking more clearly than the rest of us. It was imperative to get you away as quickly as possible and take your mother to their house. They took onboard Jusef's concerns and didn't want to put any of us at risk, more than we already were. So plans were quickly changed; Jusef contacted David and my father contacted Peer. It broke your grandmother's heart to send you away alone but it was all the money they had."

"But you said they were all rounded up from *your* house. Did Mama go back there?"

"Eventually, yes. Elise and Jusef stayed with your grandparents for a few days until they were satisfied it was safe, then came to live with us. They both still had their jobs and with a baby on the way, they needed to work. And at the time, the war was a new entity and we had no idea how long it would last or how bad it would get. Most Dutch people were still convinced it was a mistake; that Hitler hadn't meant to invade. Anyway, your mother came back briefly when Ida was born but didn't like to stay away from her parents for long, plus travelling was becoming more difficult, even that short distance. Then, not long before they were all taken, Elise became ill so your mother rushed to be by her side and in her absence, your grandparents were taken to Westerbork."

I nodded. The last part of that sentence was the only bit I already knew. I had never allowed myself to think of what life was like for them before deportation. I couldn't bear it. I couldn't add to my nightmares.

"Ezra, do you know why my father was shot?"

He shook his head, eyeing me. My tone had given me away, I knew it.

"Why, do you?" he asked.

"Yes." As soon as I said it, I instantly felt a surge of relief. Is this what confession feels like? Ezra straightened, his eyes fixed on mine.

"Go on."

"Do you remember Hannie?"

"Your best friend? Yes, I do. She always wanted me to be the handsome prince in all her games," he chuckled. "What about her?"

A flash of memory stopped me for a moment. A reluctant Ezra sitting on an upturned bucket, a red tablecloth cape wrapped round him and a wooden sword by his side. Hannie sat at his feet, a delighted grin spread across her face. She had been besotted with him.

"Kristabel, what about her?" he prompted.

"The day before it happened, I told her that we were leaving. That we were running away from the monsters. I knew it was wrong to; Papa had specifically told me not to tell anyone - that morning when they told *me* of the plan. But I didn't think Hannie was just 'anyone'; she was my best friend til death – we'd made a pact, you see. No secrets. But ..." I paused, watching his face, listening intently. "I think she went home and told her parents and they told somebody else."

"Who? And why? What would that gain?"

"I don't know but Papa always said to trust no-one. I betrayed him. It must have been me!"

"I don't think he meant *no-one.*" He regarded me for a moment. I was quite shaken by my confession – by voicing the fear that had haunted me for a lifetime. "I think you're wrong, Kristabel."

"Am I though?"

"Yes, absolutely. It makes no sense." He patted my hand, shaking his head. "Have you been torturing yourself with this for all these years?"

I nodded. "It's been my recurring nightmare, forever. Of course I blame myself; I don't understand why else he was shot or why they were there that day."

"It wasn't because of you, my dear Kristabel; not at all. They went to Auschwitz, you know – Hannie and her family."

"Did they survive?"

Ezra shook his head.

"Did you find *anybody* we knew?" I asked.

"No."

We sat in silence for a while, snippets of childhood memory lingering in our minds.

"So if it wasn't because of me, why was Papa shot?"

He sighed. It was obviously a question he had already given some thought to.

"Well, the obvious answer would be, because he was a Jew but I don't think it was that either. Yes, they marched into Poland and killed everyone in sight but it was different with our country. The Netherlands was an open door and once the government had gone, they just rolled right in. They wanted to establish some kind of order, quite peacefully, to start with. I remember my father was nervous because it was too calm. And then soon enough, it all changed. But no, Isaak's death was nothing to do with your friend."

"I don't understand, Ezra. What are you not telling me?"

"There was a rumour that Mr Gerson was a name on the Nazi's list. Somebody they wanted to remove instantly. And so, because your father stood up for him, they assumed he was also involved. I don't know; it's all speculation."

"Involved in what?"

184

"Like I said, it's a rumour, nothing substantiated. Mr Gerson's name was not in fact Gerson. He wasn't Dutch, he was Polish. And a member of the Polish Resistance, probably the Secret Army; the Underground State. The thing is, Jusef told us that the man who shot your father was wearing civilian clothes, which could mean he was with the Gestapo. And that lends some credence to the rumour. Which started my father wondering if Isaak *had* been involved in something serious. Some plot with the Resistance. Just talking about it would be enough to get yourself shot. I don't think my father or our uncles knew exactly what but they seemed to accept that Isaak had been involved in *something*. I know that he was the political one: the most outspoken. He wouldn't just sit back and accept injustice. I remember Abel once said that Isaak was the wild card in the family. And he admired him for it but I think he also feared it."

Chapter Fourteen

"Bella Bella!" Leon squeezed me so tightly, the same kind of bearhugs he always used to give us. His eyes still twinkled with the same mischievousness that I'd fallen for all those years ago. He took my face in his hands and for a moment I half expected him to kiss me but he just grinned.

"How can you not have changed! It's astonishing!"

"Leon, you old flatterer," I laughed and then accepted an equally tight hug from his wife, Janet. Fiona hadn't joined them for the journey in the end, due to a lingering cold, so was spending New Year with her son's family. Leon was free with his hugs, stopping to study Rueben's face before embracing him.

"I am delighted to meet you, Rueben. Delighted." He was also particularly thrilled to greet Chaya and Ezra, clapping him on the back and enquiring about their journey.

"Did they know about Ezra?" I asked Filip quietly.

He chuckled. "This is Sabina we're talking about; she's always told Leon everything. She doesn't keep much to herself, unless she absolutely has to."

After noisy greetings and gift giving – Janet had bought gifts for all the children, including Majbritt – and lively chatter over cups of tea, there followed similarly lively chatter over lunch. I absolutely loved listening to Leon's endless stories; his enthusiasm and dry wit took me back to the long summer days during school holidays, when he and Gabbi would tell stories and make us act them out, giving us the challenge of improvising costumes for our outlandish characters. Listening to him and Sabina now, made me realise just how much I had missed out on. They had maintained that tight bond we'd all had, and I have to admit, the pang of jealousy was almost

186

overwhelming. Looking up, I caught Rueben watching me. His smile told me he could read my thoughts all too well. I looked away only to find Ezra also watching me. His was a different kind of smile though; it was one of still coming to terms with finding me alive after nearly eighty years of mourning my untimely and brutal death.

After lunch, Ezra, Leon, Filip, Rueben and I settled by the fire in the smaller room while the others ventured into the garden to give the children a chance to let off steam. I watched for a while from the window, smiling at their shrieks of delight and bright red cheeks from the sharp cold. Ezra was in full swing, relaying more tales of his war years. Both Leon and Filip, being the same age as him, wanted to know what it'd been like for the young children to live through; what they potentially could have lived through. And Rueben was as keen as ever to glean any information about the family he'd never known.

"So, once the war had ended, what did you do?"

"I followed everybody else; I went back to Amsterdam, hoping to find my family. Anybody. Survivors were arriving from the holding camps, so I waited. But," he shrugged, shaking his head, "It soon became apparent that none of them had survived. None from Germany and certainly none from Amsterdam. So I was put on a ship for America. I had Esther's address and as far as the Red Cross were concerned, that meant I was one less child to try and rehome. I was lucky that they did that because not being a camp survivor, I slipped through the net. I wasn't processed. As far as they were concerned, I just appeared from the rubble and they scratched their heads a bit, not knowing what to do with me. So, thank goodness I had that address. I spent a few years with Esther and Abraham; they were the best kind of people.

So giving, so warm, so desperate to make up for everything I had lost. But I was restless. I'd been so used to fending for myself and then suddenly at the age of seventeen when I *should* be fending for myself, I was being smothered. So, after a few years, I went to Israel."

"Israel? Why?" Filip wondered.

"Well, I had kept in touch with a few other 'displaced' young men, and there was a job for me. Esther was upset, naturally, but she understood. *'You wouldn't be family if you didn't have the wanderlust,'* she said. So off I went, to work for Mossad." He laughed lightly at the stunned silence. "Yes I know; crazy! But it's what I *needed* to do. I felt useful, active. It wasn't just about revenge – well, no, I think it probably was – but also it was about putting to use everything I had learnt during the war. I learnt very quickly to second guess, to anticipate, to predict how certain people on the run would behave. Where they would go. How they would blend into society, undetected. I have to say, it was an exciting job. That sounds wrong, I know, but after years of being hunted and in hiding, it felt liberating to be the hunter. And then I met Chaya, fell in love and suddenly had a new perspective on life. A few years later, I left my job and we moved to America. Esther and Abraham weren't getting any younger and they didn't have children of their own, so I felt it was only right to be there for them. And I'd grown weary of fighting. Of living on the edge. It was Chaya who suggested I go into teaching. So, that's what I did. I started out teaching history but in later years I focused primarily on the Holocaust. I feel it's my duty to remind people of what happened. If we allow them to forget, it could happen again. And it has. Just look at the Bosnian war. Look at Rwanda. Darfur. Eventually, I left the classroom to travel round to schools and events, giving talks.

As you can see," he waved a dismissive hand, "I can talk for hours! But the funny thing is, despite my tales of survival and dodging the Gestapo, the thing that impresses young people the most is when I tell them I met Otto Frank."

"You did?" I sat up I my seat. "When?"

"After the war. When I went back to Amsterdam. He was just a camp survivor – one of hundreds of displaced Jews – waiting for news of his family. He wasn't famous back then. We struck up a conversation when we discovered we were both German." He watched me laugh. "What's so funny?"

"Nothing, just ... the irony. So, did we know Anne Frank?"

"No, not at all. But Otto Frank knew our fathers."

"Did he?"

"Yes. He remembered them. It makes sense though; businessmen from Germany, living and working in the same district of Amsterdam. They probably all stuck together. I don't suppose they were good friends or anything but it gave me great comfort just to find somebody who had known them."

We lapsed into silence. My mind was racing with thoughts of Ezra hunting Nazis after the war. What must it have been like for him, surviving occupation.

"Did you ever kill anybody? I asked quietly.

"Yes. Yes, I did." He watched my reaction, then glanced at the others. "Did I regret it? No. At the time, with the Resistance, I was too busy surviving, and after the war, I was too angry. I didn't care about their nationality. It was their ideology that shaped them. Turned them into murderers. I wish I'd killed more."

"That's terrible! Sad, I mean," I quickly corrected.

"Is it? I watched them take my family away. *Watched* them. I felt so useless. I let it happen."

"But what could you do?"

"Nothing. I know that now but it took a long time to forgive myself."

"For what?"

"For surviving."

I typed in that hateful name and peered at the screen, searching. Both Leon and Ezra had gone for a nap before dinner and Sabina was busy in the kitchen with an army of young helpers, so I took the opportunity to commandeer her computer for a short while. Rueben came into the room, quietly shutting the door behind him.

"Everything alright, Mama?" He looked over my shoulder at the screen and stopped short. I hadn't wanted company but at the same time, he'd know exactly what to look for.

"I want to see if I can find Howard. Or Sara Ephraim. I've never looked before but it struck me when I was listening to Ezra talk about his work and how they identified people from camp photos, and I suddenly thought, Howard might be here in these photos of the liberation."

"Right." He pulled up a chair next to me. "let's have a look then."

It's not what I'd expected. It's much, much worse. Stomach-churning. Nauseating. Panic inducing. And yet I felt compelled to look, to scrutinise.

"Have you not looked before, then?"

I shook my head. "No. I've always avoided it. I didn't want to see it, or believe it. No, not believe … I didn't want to know."

"But …"

"I know. Shameful."

"No, that's not what I was going to say at all. I understand you don't want to face how they died, or where they died, but if it were me, I wouldn't be able to rest knowing there may be photos of them somewhere."

"What do you mean?"

"You're looking at Belsen for photos of Howard but what about all the other camps? For photos of your family."

Too much. The thought made me lightheaded. "I couldn't possibly, Rueben. I couldn't bear that."

He nodded. "Okay, yes. Understood. And you're right; that would be too much. I suppose for me, it's different because I didn't actually know them. I'm sorry, Mama."

"Don't be. I'm a coward, I know it. I never admitted who I was or what my religion was. I was embarrassed. Guilty. I thought, if I met a survivor of the camps, what would they think of me? I sat it out in luxury – okay, a damp, cold, luxury – but compared to what they went through, it was heaven. I felt like I had no right to say, I'm a Jew. A Dutch Jew. In reality, I'm just a fake. I used to wish they hadn't sent me away. I wished I had died with them. Or survived, but *really* survived; lived the horror and survived. Like Ezra. I can't say I did that. Not at all. I lost my family, yes, but they lost their lives."

"Mama…"

"And if Ezra couldn't forgive himself, how on earth can I?"

Rueben put his arm around me. "I don't know what to say. You can't torture yourself about the past; surely we've both learnt that much, no?"

"I know. But somehow I feel I should." We stared at each other. He could tell I wasn't meaning just about the war. I turned back to the screen. "This is horrific. Are all the photos as bad?"

"Mama, this is the liberation. This is distressing but maybe don't look any further. I can search for Howard, if you'd like?"

I took in a deep breath. "Sit with me. Let's look together."

I sat down heavily on the bed in one of the guest rooms designated for me, closing my eyes. The images didn't go away. The endless row of haunted, emaciated faces. I reached for Howard's hand next to me.

"I think we found you today; I'm sure it was you. By one of the barracks. You were crouching, talking to a figure hunched on the ground, squatting among the dead. There were bodies everywhere. How on earth did you cope with that?"

"I didn't want you to see that."

"I know. But I needed to. You protected me so well. Too well."

"*Too* well?"

"I wish you'd talked about it to me. It would have helped me come to terms with it, I think."

"I couldn't. That was, unequivocally, the worst time of my entire life. It affected me so deeply. It made me ill for years; it traumatised me. And to think your mother died there – I didn't want you to know."

"I thought I saw her too. I was looking for her in the sea of faces but of course, she was already dead. And she would've been unrecognisable, Rueben said. I think he's right. I can't imagine."

"I don't want you to imagine. Kristabel, don't try to. Just treasure your memories of her; of them all. Don't search for ghosts amidst the hideousness of war."

I looked up at our reflection in the wardrobe mirror at the foot of the bed. Only I stared back.

"I wish you were here, Howard."

My mind's brimming over with things I need to share, need to talk about. Rueben and I watched some incredibly distressing footage of the liberation of Belsen. We listened to first-hand accounts from young men – probably friends of Howard – as they described what horrors they were confronted with and how they set about trying to help the thousands that had survived. I say, *survived* – thousands were barely alive and thousands died even after liberation, from disease and starvation. Indiscriminate piles of bodies stacked up throughout the camp; some not yet dead, tangled up with the very dead. It was the liberators job to examine the packed barracks and try to identify there which were dead and which were living, and then separate them. Image upon image, account upon account of unimaginable horrors, of a fearsome stench from which there was no escape. It pervaded everything. Of an eerie stillness. No sounds, no movement, no commotion. No cries of pain or anguish. No cheers at being liberated. Just the stillness of death.

I'm not sure why I decided to look up Belsen today. Maybe it was listening to Ezra that spurred me on. Hearing about how he escaped the camps by the skin of his teeth and then spent the years after the war helping to track down the perpetrators.

There was a knock at the door. It was Sabina.

"You're awake! Did you manage an afternoon nap?"

I shook my head. "You?"

"I just had ten minutes in the chair. Leon's snoring – can you hear him?" She cocked her head, listening, smiling.

"How about the others?"

"I think everybody crashed out for a little while. It was a late night last night, wasn't it? Zofia took the children next door so they could either nap or settle with a film for a bit."

"Has she always lived next door to you?" I asked, patting the bed for her to sit next to me.

"No. After she and Matthew got married they moved away, to the Cotswolds. Absolutely loved it! But then when she fell pregnant she wanted to come home, so they sold up and moved nearer. Then about twenty years ago, next door went on the market and they snapped it up. And their children have all stayed in the area, so I get to see them all the time. And since Zofia retired, she's been a childminder for her grandchildren. She loves it. I love it too because there's always children running around, getting under our feet. It keeps us young." She smiled awkwardly, realising suddenly she may be touching on a nerve. "How are you and Rueben? I was coming through with cake earlier but I saw you two deep in conversation and I didn't want to intrude."

"Yes, we're fine. It was a little rocky at first but I think we will be fine. This has helped, being here with all of you. And Ezra!" I clutched her hand. "Thank you; thank you for that!"

"Yes, I wept when Filip told me Marta had found him. I can't tell you how difficult it was to keep it secret! Ordinarily, I would've told you straight away but you had enough on your plate getting to know Rueben, so I left it until Ezra could actually be here. He's marvellous, isn't he! And with so many stories to tell. I find it fascinating but every now and then, it suddenly hits me that that could have so easily been our world too. Don't you think?"

We sat in silence for a while. "Are you sure you're okay?" she asked.

I sighed heavily. "I feel a failure, Sabina. An all-round failure. I failed my parents by not shouting about their murder. I failed Rueben – I'm still failing him. I refused to patch things

194

up for so many years because his wife is German, and it turns out, so am I!"

"And Inge? What's she like?"

"The best! The absolute best kind of daughter-in-law anyone could wish for."

"Well then. Put it behind you."

"And I think I failed Howard."

"How?"

"By not being completely truthful. I never talked about *you* for a start. So of course, I failed you too. You, Marta, Leon – all of you."

She didn't argue, she just studied me with those honest, steady eyes. "But how did you fail Howard? I thought you two were happy."

"Oh, we were. But I think, with hindsight, when he said he didn't want to talk about Belsen because it would upset me too much, I took that to mean he didn't want to talk about *any* of it; what he went through during the war. The horrors. So I didn't talk either. I ignored it. Neither of us wanted to face the truth."

"None of us *wanted* to face the truth – it was a case of having to."

"But we didn't, you see. Not at all. We hid from it. And now I wonder whether he needed to talk but didn't think I'd want to hear about it. And I've never faced it because I didn't want to upset him. What a mess, Sabina; what a mess."

"But Bella, listen to yourself! You've been saying all long how you don't look back; you just focus on the now, the future. And here you are with Ezra and Rueben, and Inge, and you're just focusing on what you didn't talk to Howard about. You can't do anything about it. Not now." She gave me an almighty hug. "Go and embrace your future!"

195

"What's left of it."

"Well then! Make the most of it."

I sat for a while longer after she'd left the room, staring at my reflection. I'd never realised before just how self-centred I am. Honestly, it had never struck me. Here I am, feeling sorry for myself about the holocaust, about what I lost. Feeling guilty for living out the war over here. Oh, poor me! Everybody is rallying round me, checking if I'm alright, worrying that I've been upset by Ezra's tales of families being exterminated. It didn't dawn on me that Sabina, Filip and Leon went through the same things. The same loss. The same guilt. They're not making a fuss. Rueben has lived his life parentless too but not because he's an orphan. He's not making a fuss.

'Get a grip, Kristabel!' I scowled at my reflection. I wonder if I'll ever like myself. Will I ever look in the mirror and instinctively smile back at me? I've been happy in life, don't get me wrong. But not happy with me. Other people have made me happy and I'd like to think I've reciprocated – I hope I have. I hope I made Howard happy. No, I know I did; I'm sure of that much. I made a mess of friendships but in the time that I had them, I hope I made my friends happy too. And we are reconnecting in such a way that fills me with an excitement for the future.

I can honestly say, I have never been one to self-analyse or evaluate my life as I have in the past two months. It has been quite an eye-opener – a revelation. And a much-needed one at that. I have my friends to thank for that. I feel a long list of New Year's resolutions coming on. Maybe this time I'll make a concerted effort to keep them.

"Okay everybody, move in closer. That's it. Hanna, budge up to Majbritt a bit more. Great! Smile! Everybody say *cheese*!"

"Cheese, Sabina?" Leon retorted. "No, no, where we come from we say *Shalom!*"

"*Shalom!*" we all chorused, laughing as we held glasses aloft to salute one another after grinning at Sabina's phone, hovering before us on a selfie stick.

"Thank you, that's fantastic. I'll send that to Marta in a bit; she will be thrilled to see us all together." Sabina put her phone down and clapped her hands together. "Okay people, dig in!" We all took the same seats as lunch, vocalising our appreciation at the lavish spread before us. Sabina had opted to cook a repeat of their Christmas dinner along with all the trimmings, and more.

"Do you ever stop feeding?" Leon commented, piling slices of meat on to his plate.

"Absolutely not!" Sabina laughed. "Why on earth would I do that?"

Crackers pulled, hats placed at jaunty angles, jokes read and laughed at, followed by a contented hush as we started to eat.

"What's your favourite Christmas memory?" Leon piped up, instigating the conversation. "Or Hanukkah, if you'd prefer. I've celebrated both since I came to England; I know most of you have too. Filip, let's start with you." And so the story telling began again. We all followed Filip's lead, keeping it light and fun, however poignant. It was soon my turn.

"My first mince pie and brandy butter. I begged for seconds because I was convinced I would get drunk on the butter!"

"And did you?" Jan laughed.

"Of course not! I was very disappointed."

"Oh my goodness, I remember that!" Sabina exclaimed, her chuckle becoming an unstoppable guffaw at the memory. "Oh, Bella, that was so funny. We were desperate to be grown-ups, weren't we!"

When it came to Rueben's turn I was expecting him to say his first Christmas as a father or a husband. I was suddenly acutely aware at the lack of happy childhood memories he had and couldn't look at him.

"My first Christmas in England, with Mama and Howard." He turned and raised his glass to me, a wonderfully rare, unabashed smile on his face. "And yes, we had brandy butter and no, Mama did not get drunk on it then, either." Everybody roared with laughter again. He held my eye for a breathtakingly long time, that smile unwavering. I caught Inge out of the corner of my eye dabbing at her lashes with a tissue. *'Thank you'*, I mouthed to him. He nodded, pleased.

"I have a new memory to share," Annika said, when everybody had finished their turn. "Well, we both do," she smiled at Jan. We all turned to them, waiting. I knew it! I could tell. I shot a look at Majbritt, busy playing with the miniature bowling set she had won in her Christmas cracker, seemingly unaware of the expectant hush – pardon the pun.

"We will be greeting a new addition to our family, in April. The twenty-first, if he's on time!"

"*He*?" we all chorused and got up from our seats to hug her and Jan in turn. Suddenly aware of the attention her mother was getting, Majbritt jumped up from her seat next to Hanna and ran round to Annika, wriggling onto her lap and smiling brightly.

The meal ended with animated talk about babies, grandchildren and great grandchildren, and the year ahead with everything it promised to bring. Annika basked in the attention she received, happy to have finally shared her secret but Majbritt looked distinctly dejected. Her initial bright smile had faded and a worried frown replaced it. When we all left the table, I beckoned her to follow me into the lounge. She climbed onto my lap, smoothing down her dress as she always did.

"You look very pretty, Majbritt; I do love that dress." She was wearing the same one she'd worn to the theatre. She stroked the sleeve of my forest green, velvet dress.

"You look pretty too, Grandma. We look like princesses."

"We do," I smiled. "Fancy a game of snap?" I offered her the miniature pack of cards I'd won in my cracker. Her face lit up. I'm not sure she fully understands the concept of snap but it kept her happy for a while, snatching up every pair of cards dealt, regardless of colour or suit.

"So, how do you feel about being a big sister?"

Majbritt shrugged. "Mamma says it will be wonderful for me."

"I think Mamma is absolutely right. You will be a fantastic big sister."

She leant against my chest, deep in thought. "Did you have a brother?"

"No."

"A sister then?"

"No."

"Oh." She looked worried.

"But I had lots of cousins. And Ezra was like a brother to me; so I can imagine it *will* be wonderful for you. A friend to play with, to read stories to. And I'm sure you can help to decorate the bedroom, ready for the new baby." That cheered her up. She straightened, eyes wide, beaming at me.

"You can help me! We can make it pretty and we can get lots of teddies."

"We can," I agreed. And with that, she slid from my lap and ran to bombard Annika with all her thoughts on the décor.

The rest of the evening was very relaxed, with Sabina handing round plates of cake and bowls of nuts. I don't think I have ever eaten as much food as I have over the past two days. I said as much to Sabina but she just waved a dismissive hand and laughed, offering to top up my glass.

Leon and Ezra were still regaling us with stories of farming and teaching alike, not once mentioning the war years again, for which I was very grateful. *Frozen* was on the television in the other room and we were treated to an impromptu song and dance routine from Hanna, Ola and Majbritt. It amazed me how coordinated they were considering they'd had zero rehearsal time, until Zofia pointed out that every girl under the age of ten knows this routine off by heart.

"Oh, I see," I nodded, "Disney films have just passed me by, I'm afraid. I really feel like I've missed out on something."

"You really haven't," Zofia chuckled. "When you've watched *Frozen* as many times as I have, you'd give anything just to not have that song replaying in your head all day. Even in your sleep, sometimes!"

I watched the girls giving it their all and found myself wondering what Lena's child – my great grandchild – would grow up to be like. And Lena; had she watched Disney films as a child? Had she also done this; delighted her parents with dance routines from her favourite films? I smiled at Ezra and Chaya, both singing along as they watched. Janet too. It was clear I was the only one in the room who hadn't been exposed to the contagion that is, *Let it Go*.

By midnight, despite their insistence to the contrary, both Hanna and Majbritt had fallen fast asleep; one sprawled on the sofa, the other curled up on one of the armchairs. Ola had been put to bed in Sabina's room but Paul and Nik – the youngest two – were wide awake and refreshed from their earlier nap. We all gathered in a circle by the fire, counting down along with the television, glass in hand, ready to toast in the New Year. I looked round at the jubilant faces; at my oldest friends, at my favourite cousin, at my son, and had an overwhelming urge to weep. A cheer went up and we all hugged and kissed each other.

"Raise your glasses to twenty-nineteen," Leon called. We held them high. "To Arno," he said. "And Gabbi."

"To Mrs Trigg," Sabina continued.

"To the Ruebensteins," Ezra smiled.

"And the Van Dijks," I added. "My grandparents."

"To all our grandparents. To all our parents," Filip continued.

"And to Howard," Rueben said. And *that's* when I did weep. Nothing dramatic, just an unstoppable stream of tears, for the second day running. But they were tears of happiness. Happy that we were all together to remember them. To hold them close in our hearts, always.

Chapter Fifteen

"Good morning, Bella!" I opened my eyes to find Sabina placing a cup of tea on the bedside unit. "Did you sleep well?"

"Mmm, yes, I did, thank you. You?"

"Out like a light." It had been after one by the time we had all said our goodnights. Leon and Janet stayed next door at Zofia's, with Annika and Jan. Hanna had been sleeping over too, sharing a room with Majbritt. Rueben, Inge, Ezra, Chaya and I were all staying with Sabina.

"It's been wonderful having everybody here. Is this what you do every New Year?" I propped myself up, making room for her to sit next to me.

"Well, Leon and Janet used to come down or we'd go up there when our children were younger. But yes, all the grandchildren and their little ones come over. What about you? Did Howard have family?"

"Not really. It was just us usually. But that's how we liked it," I added, spying a look of pity on her face. That's not strictly true but what we really wanted hadn't been an option. Until now.

Annika, Jan and Majbritt left after a late breakfast, amid promises of coming back soon, and keeping Zofia up to date with pregnancy progress reports. Majbritt and Hanna clung to each other like life-long friends. Majbritt turned and waved at me.

"Goodbye, Grandma!" Then she ran and threw herself at Sabina, hugging her tightly. "Goodbye, other Grandma!"

Sabina chuckled. "Goodbye, Majbritt. Thank you for the lovely pictures you painted for me. See you again soon." We waved until their car was out of sight.

"Tea and cake anybody, before I do lunch?"

"But Sabina, we've just eaten!" I clutched my stomach to emphasise the point.

"You know what your trouble is, Bella – you eat like a sparrow!"

"Surely you mean a mouse? I think sparrows are very greedy, aren't they?"

She feigned annoyance. "Whatever! You don't eat enough and I bet you skip meals when you're on your own."

She wasn't wrong but I wasn't going to give her the satisfaction of letting her know. She tucked her arm through mine as we walked to the door. "Never mind, you're all here for another four days. Plenty of time to make sure you eat properly," she teased.

"Good grief, you'll be rolling me out of the house by then!" We burst out laughing, nudging each other with our elbows.

"Is this what these two were like as young girls, Leon?" Rueben asked, smiling at our infantile behaviour. Leon raised his eyes to the heavens.

"Rueben, they were an absolute handful! Always joking about, always teasing each other. And when rationing was over, I've never known anybody eat as much cake as your mother."

"I did not!"

" Yes, you did! And ice-cream. And eggs." He shook his head in mock despair. I laughed.

"Yes, well, it had been a long war. Cake was always my favourite," I defended.

"Well then, what are you complaining about?" Sabina interjected. "Tea and cake it is!"

"Where are they off to?" I watched Ezra and Rueben walk down the drive.

"Just to the shop to fetch some milk," Sabina replied airily. "Did you need milk?"

"I always need milk!" she smiled. As I said, she's a terrible liar. And she knows it. "I think they just wanted some time alone, that's all."

"Whatever for?" I wondered. She shrugged, then busied herself clearing the table of cups and plates. I followed her into the kitchen. Inge was showing Chaya and Janet the photos of Isaak and Lena, and Filip and Leon were locked in a battle on the chess board. I felt quite superfluous. I don't know why I was fretting about Rueben and Ezra disappearing for a chat; it wasn't as if I had anything left to hide. I'd already told Ezra about my disastrous attempt at motherhood and the consequent estrangement. I need to stop worrying – I have no secrets left. Even so, I gave Ezra a searching look on their return nearly an hour later. He smiled and put his arm round me.

"You have a wonderful son, Kristabel."

"I know. Why, what did he say?"

"He just wanted to make sure that you'd been truthful about the past; about your relationship with him."

"But I was!" What could Rueben mean by that?

"Relax; what he meant was, whether you'd told me what an unbelievably difficult person he'd been to live with. How he had tormented you and Howard, and how he'd tried to drive a wedge between the pair of you, and how he had pushed you to breaking point. Intentionally. Maliciously."

I just stared at him.

"You didn't tell me *that* now, did you? Rueben wanted me to be absolutely clear on the facts. You weren't a bad mother;

he was a bad son. A lost son. A son bent on destruction. And from what I can gather, a son who has been tormenting himself about it ever since."

"But … he's been so angry with me."

"Yes, but a lot of that anger is at himself too. You know this already but he just wanted *me* to be aware of it, too. I think he was asking for my forgiveness, in a strange way."

"*You're* forgiveness?"

"He just didn't want me to think badly of you. Which I don't."

Just then, Zofia and Matthew arrived.

"We've dropped Hanna back home. She was quite tearful after Majbritt left, bless her. And Ola had been sick in the night; too much excitement yesterday." Zofia turned to Sabina. "Any chance of a cuppa, Mum? It's been quite a morning!"

"Absolutely! Tea and cake coming right up."

And that set the tone for the next four days. Rueben and Inge, Ezra and Chaya, Leon and Janet, and me, along with our hosts Sabina, Filip, Zofia and Matthew, spent the time talking, eating and above all, laughing together. We went for a blustery walk around the village one morning, we had lunch at the local pub one afternoon, and we made use of Sabina's much-loved Skype service. We Skyped Marta in New York, Isaak and Lena in Düsseldorf, Fiona in Comrie, and Ezra's sons Max and Alek, also in New York.

We grew so close in such a short amount of time, getting to know each other inside out but all too soon, the day came for us all to leave. Leon and Janet were the first to go. I hated saying goodbye. We promised to keep in touch; by phone and Skype. Getting Skype installed was now top of my list of things to do. Matthew drove them to Gatwick, with Filip along for company. Once they were back, we set off in two cars for Heathrow. I travelled in the back of Zofia's car with Rueben and Inge, and Sabina in the front. We barely spoke. It was like a heavy cloud had descended, rending us mute. I stared out of the window, watching snatches of landscape flash by in the rain. Even the weather was feeling our mood. I glanced at Rueben and mustered a smile. He raised his eyebrows. He was waiting for an answer but I couldn't give one. Not yet.

He had taken me completely by surprise after we'd waved Leon and Janet off. He had ushered me into the deserted lounge, pushing the door to behind him.

"I have a question; well, a proposition, actually."

"Oh?"

"Yes." He gave me a long, searching look. "Come and live with us in Düsseldorf, Mama."

I stared at him. He was serious! "I can't. I can't leave Howard." I hated how his face dropped; his eyes darkened with rejection. Why did I say that? Why not say anything except, *'I can't'*.

"But, he's gone. We're your family now and we want to look after you." He paused, sensing I was about to object to that. "We want to share our lives with you. And Düsseldorf is your home; it's in your blood." There was a painfully long silence as I grappled with what to say. I could feel him closing off.

"I'll think about it. It's a big move, Rueben."

"Please do. I don't want to leave you again but my home is Germany. Our children are there; our whole life is there. And I want to take you with me."

I sat down, suddenly feeling quite weak. He sat next to me, perched at an angle.

"Mama, I understand it's all a bit sudden but," he looked me straight in the eye. "I'm scared. I didn't know how I would react to seeing you again but now I can't bear the thought of leaving you here, because…"

"Because?"

"We don't know how much time we have left."

"None of us do."

He sighed heavily. "Mama, please. Don't make me spell it out."

Just then Sabina stuck her head round the door. "Would you like something to eat before we set off, Rueben?"

"No, thank you," he smiled. She nodded, mouthed *'okay'* and disappeared again.

"Just promise you will think about it, please. I can arrange everything. We have plenty of room for whatever you wish to bring. Furniture, belongings, anything."

I stared at the carpet. I couldn't look at him. His pleading was making me panic. I didn't want him to leave – I had been dreading this day – but I just hadn't expected this. And now, I felt racked with guilt at not giving him the response he was hoping for.

At the airport, Ezra clung to me.

"Let me know which dates you decide on," he said over my head to Rueben. We'd already discussed a trip to New York to meet Ezra's family; it was just working out the logistics of travel so that I could travel with Rueben and Inge. America seems a long way away. I went there once, with Howard, many years ago. We spent a week in New York. If only I had known back then what I know now.

Saying goodbye to Rueben and Inge was even harder. I struggled to hold back tears but managed just about. Inge had no such qualms; tears were streaming down her face as she gave us all the biggest hugs.

"Phone me as soon as you arrive. It doesn't matter what time it is," I said as they walked away. Rueben nodded. He smiled but I could see that internal struggle. He suddenly looked like a seven-year-old again. I spontaneously hurried back over to hug him once more. He laughed in surprise.

"I love you, Rueben," I whispered in his ear.

"I love you too, Mama," he whispered back. And then he was gone. And then I cried.

I turned on the sidelights in the lounge and looked round the room, listening. Not a sound to be heard. All the windows had been shut tight before I left, so not even the noise of traffic was filtering through. Zofia and Sabina hadn't stayed long; just long enough to help with my luggage up the stairs, and to call in briefly on Annika on their way out, to let her know I was back. I stood by the window, staring out into darkness. It used to settle me; now, it just made me feel uneasy.

Selecting one of the Neil Diamond albums, I played our favourite track, *Say Maybe.* I picked up the framed photo of Howard and started to dance with it clutched to my chest. I closed my eyes, swaying to the music. Howard wrapped his arms around me and kissed my hair. I smiled and sighed a contented sigh.

"Oh, Howard, what do I do?" He didn't answer. We just kept dancing. "I know, I know; I need to figure this one out myself. But how?" We danced for a while in silence, content in each other's arms.

"It's time, Kristabel." I could feel his breath in my ear as he whispered.

"Time for what?"

He sighed. "You know what. It's time to let me go."

"But I don't want to!" I whimpered, tightening my hold of him.

"I know, but you must, my darling. It'll be alright now."

I opened my eyes, blinking in the semi-dark. I looked at the photo I was holding. He silently smiled back at me. That smile will never change.

Three weeks later

Today's a big day for me. Jack will be here in a while to collect Howard's clothes. I've kept a few things; his favourite cardigan, the jacket, a novelty Christmas tie I bought him just to see his face, which he then wore every year just to tease me, but everything else is going to a refugee crisis centre that Annika put me on to. It seemed appropriate and I know Howard would definitely approve.

I'm not moving on; I'm moving out. It is the obvious choice. I'm moving to Düsseldorf, to live with Rueben and Inge. I wish I'd jumped at the invitation from the onset – it's what my heart was telling me to do – but I needed to give it some careful thought first. My biggest concern was leaving Howard behind but as Annika quite rightly pointed out, he will come with me, in spirit. He wouldn't let me go on my own. He will always be with me, wherever I go. Only his tombstone will be here and Annika has promised to take care of that for me. Or I pay somebody to manage it if it gets too much for her. My future is with Rueben. And that is such a great feeling.

Next month, the three of us are travelling to New York for a fortnight, to meet our family over there. And to see Marta. Dear Marta; without her, Ezra and I would never have known the truth about each other. Imagine! And in June, once Annika and the baby are settled into a routine, they will all come over to Germany to stay with us. I'm excited to show them where my family came from. I haven't even been there myself yet but I just know it will be perfect. Emotional but perfect. Fitting.

I worried about leaving Annika just as she's entering a new and important phase in life but a curious thing has happened; Annika and Zofia have struck up a strong friendship. Zofia has

210

called over to see her every week since the New Year, which has meant I've seen Sabina as often too. I think Zofia will make a far better companion and substitute mother than I ever could for Annika, so I am happy. And I can start a life with Rueben and Inge knowing Annika and Majbritt will be fine.

I may even visit Amsterdam with Rueben – we discussed it last night briefly, over the phone. I dearly want to visit Lena's grave one more time, and see where I grew up, through different eyes now. Older, wiser eyes. Eyes that are no longer lost or frightened. I may even visit Auschwitz to pay my respects; I know Rueben wants to. I feel I've come full circle. As Howard said, it's time.

And tomorrow I will be giving a talk at Majbritt's school as part of the Holocaust commemorations. It's a big step for me. I had to read up on the events of the war in Europe. On the Holocaust. I know it sounds ridiculous but I needed to make sure I had my facts right. And the more I read, the more I realised how little I actually knew. I was there, watching my family avidly read the papers and listen to the news, and yet, it passed me by. I didn't see it coming. Not at all. Not until that day. That image will never leave me. How I have wished over the years for a different image to be the one I remember of my darling Papa but I've come to realise, it is what it is. Regardless of how I remember them, the fact remains that they did everything to protect me, to shield me from the horrors unfolding around us, and then my mother saved me, knowing she couldn't save herself.

I can't say *I survived* because I didn't endure what so many did. I lived out the war in the safety of England. I *lived*. I still live. And tomorrow, I am going to honour the countless who don't. There's not a day goes by when I don't think about my family. When I don't kiss their picture 'good morning' and 'good night'. It has been a private grief; not one I have wanted to share or shout about. But tomorrow, I am finally letting them out of the box and into the hearts and minds of those eager young children, excited to hear my story. I know they're excited because Majbritt told me so. And she is the most honest best friend I have ever had.

***

THE END

Acknowledgements

With special thanks to my cousin Anthony who shared his Dutch side of the family tree with me, which ended in Auschwitz and Sobibor.

As ever, a massive thank you to my family, Team Griffiths – Simon, Carina, Dino, Anton, Lou, Damon & Heidi – for your unfailing support and love. Thanks also to my feline trio for all the cuddles.
To my family & friends, my Facebook family and my readers; 2020 has been a challenging year for us all. Thank you for being there and keeping each other sane.
Thank you, Neil Diamond – you legend. Thank you, Spotify. Thank you, NHS. For everything.

Out now

When the father of her eighteen-year-old daughter walked back into her life, Alice knew she was in trouble. She had kept their child a secret after he disappeared with her best friend, leaving her in the lurch and broken hearted. But now he seemed intent on picking up where they left off.

The consequences were far greater than she could have possibly imagined; exposing dark secrets, harboured grudges and a web of deceit that ensured life would never be the same again.

Cobbled Streets & Teenage Dreams is a tale of forbidden love, lies and loss, spanning three generations. It follows the painful journey of four women as they come to terms with the past in order to confront the present.

Coming soon

When the tanks start to arrive in the New Forest, the residents of Brockenhurst just know their village is once again going to play a part in the war. Life had barely got back to normal since the end of the last one. For three local brothers, Reg, Fred and Bert Greene, the Second World War was about to change their lives forever and tear their world apart.

Whispering Trees, book three of the *Cobbled Streets* saga, follows the brothers fate as they enlist to fight in the campaign in Europe, leaving loved ones and childhood behind.

Also coming soon

Brianna has the perfect life; happily married with a job she loves, beautiful home in the country and three successful children away at university. She's embracing hitting fifty – after all, everybody knows that's when life really begins. Then fate deals her a blow that unravels her perfect world so fast and leaves her fighting for her life. The one person that comes to her aid is the same person she's trying to avoid, but quickly realises she can't live without.

Anam Cara is a tale of love, loss, strength and endurance against all odds.

Printed in Great Britain
by Amazon